THE RAYS ON
DAYSTAR HAVEN

UNIESQUE

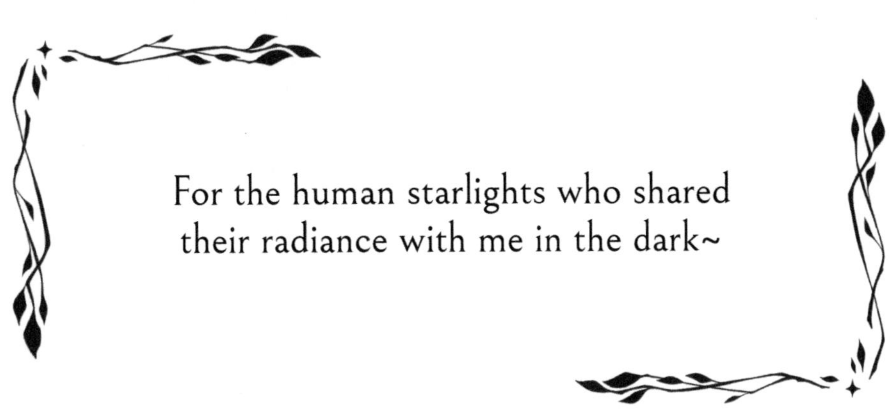

For the human starlights who shared
their radiance with me in the dark~

TABLE OF CONTENTS

CHAPTER I

Five years of the sweetest torment imaginable. Twenty seasons of bliss with a bitter aftertaste, and she'd lost count of the star-kissed days that inevitably gave way to the shroud of malice every twenty-four hours.

Yet, that was home.

The slow descent of the daystar behind an impenetrable veil of a blackening forest marked the end of another day in refuge and the onset of Elunai's unrest. This happened consistently at every turn of the day into night, yet no passage of time seemed to sate the young woman's tension.

A previously held breath passed through her lips as the final ray vanished, leaving the remnants of twilight lingering over the surrounding tree tops. Head lowering, Elunai's viridescent gaze made its way across the clearing, taking in the darkening aura.

A small, wet nose nudged her cheek, and she clutched the lit torch in her hand a bit more tightly. "Why can't the night stars be brighter...at least for this part?" she mused to the ivory wisp of fur on her shoulder.

"Keep it lit," the squirrel replied, his tone curt, yet low. He knew this was her most detested part of the evening, but the lamps had to burn.

Every night, without fail, those fires would light, or their world would be devoured. All two acres of it.

The maiden pressed her lips shut, muscles tensing throughout her body as she resisted voicing the rebuttal she knew would be quickly dismissed. Elunai's jaw shifted as she compelled herself into forward movement. Legs stiff, she made her way through the garden and across the clearing, first to the southern edge.

Two, lightly carved, timber posts stood on each side of the stone path before a break in the trees that led into the abyss of the wooded world. Large lanterns awaiting their flame hung from simple, iron fixtures attached to each post. The dim stillness of the lamps seemed sinfully contrary to their given purpose and invited a haste to their lighting.

"Eyes on the fire," the squirrel said firmly as the two companions neared the lanterns at the forest border.

"I know..." Elunai's whisper wavered only slightly. Their routine wasn't a practice of lamp lighting as much as it was an exercise in keeping her focus off the foreboding tree line. A sharpness gripped her chest as she raised her arm to light the first lantern.

Almost immediately, a sudden chill whipped through the darkening branches above and lashed at the skin of her outstretched hand, nearly causing her to drop the torch. With a deep breath, Elunai reinforced her will to keep her attention on the task in front of her.

The first lamp sprang to light, and the coldness lifted from the maiden's forearm as quickly as it had come. Caressing her wrist with her free hand, she turned to the second post.

"Good and strong, kid. You've got this," her albino friend said.

The second lamp was always much easier with protection from the light of the first. With a steadier hand, Elunai raised her torch to the old lantern and brought it to glorious, fiery life. She lingered a moment to let the healing heat flush her cheeks before closing the glass compartment and stepping back.

One more round.

The duo looked to the eastern clearing entrance across the meadow.

Sensing the girl's hesitation, the little one spoke again, "There's still time before complete dark. Let's go."

Elunai had often considered lighting the lamps earlier in the evening to avoid the hell of just barely finishing the task before nightfall. However, the oil supply rations wouldn't sustain if they had to burn much longer than the darkness itself.

The second and final set of lampposts stood just before a log footbridge that extended over the brook along one edge of the glade.

The girl paused at the bridge's threshold. Her eyes were glued intently on the lanterns, but something about the woods just beyond the stream dominated the attention of her remaining senses.

"Elunai," her companion said, "focus."

Was it the shadows growing naturally in the coming of night? Or was something actually...moving?

Gradient locks of copper and blonde spilled over her shoulders as the young woman leaned forward, her line of sight finally giving way to the other end of the bridge. The next moment, her head began to swim and blurred her vision. The trees appeared to wave and morph before her, causing her to stumble in a partial loss of balance.

"Elunai!" The squirrel shrieked.

Weak...

The young woman jerked back at the sudden, foreign voice ringing through her mind. Her free palm came up to press against her brow, willing the raspy word to leave her head. Her breath returned in labored gasps. Forcing her feet to move in the direction of the lamp on the right, Elunai pulled the iron and glass compartment wide open and pushed the flame of her torch against the wick. Light flooded the area.

Having stabilized against the post, the maiden turned her back to the woods and side-stepped her way to the other lamp. The shadows were already settling.

With the second lantern alight, a quiet peace moved in to replace the turmoil that had begun to stir both in and around the girl.

She lowered her head momentarily and stared at the dim gravel at her feet, allowing her trembling to abate. With a sound swallow, Elunai spun and took a giant step toward the stream, swiped the lit end of the torch through the surface waters, and started back toward the small abode at the northern end of the clearing. Her hand moved to her chest as the heartbeat faded in her ears.

"Breathe..." came the steady voice from her shoulder.

Before she could address him, the rodent abruptly turned and began sniffing the air in the direction of the bridge.

Elunai's gaze darted to the left where his had, keeping her line of sight on the ground as to avoid the trees. "What is it?" she asked.

"An animal," he responded, "just over there."

As soon as the words left him, a slight movement drew the girl's attention. Her eyes widened.

The tiny creature conjured one, final effort to pull itself from the plank walkway and collapsed under the glowing lampposts. Almost as soon as it did, Elunai's hand rested lightly upon its back.

"What's wrong...what happened?" she asked.

The chipmunk couldn't answer. Her breath was labored, eyes half closed in exhaustion.

"She's fading," the squirrel said.

The young woman's gut twisted into a nauseating knot. She tried to keep hushed, but the cry came sharp, "No...no...please, not this!" Elunai gathered the small soul into a cradle she formed from her mid-length, wrap cape and ran for the cottage, tossing the wet torch through the door of the field stable on her way.

Nearly out of her own breath by the time she clambered up the wooden steps to the door, Elunai all but fell onto the floorboards of the modest cottage's front room.

Her friend hopped off her shoulder and pushed the door closed behind them as the maiden grabbed a tattered book from one of the many supply shelves on the wall. Making her way to the large rug spread before the glowing fireplace, Elunai laid her weakening guest atop the soft fibers. Then, removing her cape, she lightly covered the chipmunk with the edge of the garment to provide a quiet solace.

Her white-coated companion found a perch on the hearth, quietly watching the girl flip as quickly as she could through thick, browning pages.

"Stay with me…" she whispered, "*Stay…!*"

Her finger landed on a block of text. Looking over at the small, barely breathing bundle on the floor before her, Elunai once again placed her hand over it and began praying in an inaudible voice.

Pale, albino eyes drifted up to the fire-lit glimmer of an eight-pointed star brooch hanging from a peg on the mantle. His gaze moved between the silver piece and the girl as if anticipatory.

Still deep in prayer, Elunai held that symbol of light and hope in her own mind as though everything depended on it. "Please…" she breathed.

"Elunai…" she heard her friend say.

That's when she realized the rising and falling under the hem of the cape had slowed to almost nothing.

Shaking her head with stinging, liquid emotion lining her eyes, the girl pulled back the cloth just enough to behold the innocent life one more time. Her form arched over the chipmunk in the most protective posture she could assume, tears spilling into the rug.

"I've got you. You're safe. You're not alone."

The squirrel winced at the familiar phrases as he listened to Elunai's hushed cries. Those words...always her final, desperate promise before...

Stillness.

"Fehln..." Her voice was weak and broken, and her stare didn't leave the floor.

He moved from the stone hearth and placed a paw atop her hand. "You did all you could, kid," he said.

"Why...am I never enough...?"

"Honestly, I think you're as you should be. And I think you need to believe that."

The limp hand balled into a fist as Elunai slowly sat back up to glare at the brooch. "Yeah...right..."

Fehln dropped his gaze, knowing full well that conversation was going nowhere fruitful. There seemed to be only one soul in existence she would truly heed, and they hadn't seen that particular traveler come through the glade in ages.

"Try to rest," he said, "I'll keep watch over this vessel until we can bury her in the morning."

CHAPTER 2

A tired hand laced through Elunai's bangs and rubbed against her still-closed eyes as the other pushed her lazily out of bed. Her movements were slow. Sleep had nearly evaded her that night.

Her bare feet shuffled softly across the wood flooring until she made her way back into the front room where her eyes couldn't help but take in the tiny, unmoving form next to Fehln and then the glint of the brooch on the mantle. An exhausted gaze melted into a glare before she turned to prepare herself for the day.

The simple act of freshening up with a round of stretches poured a bit more life into the maiden's step; however, she kept her mind relatively detached from reality until the burial was complete.

The early morning slipped away in a blur, and Elunai soon found herself kneeling under the apple blossoms before a tiny, freshly covered grave. Her hands were stained with dewy dirt, and the scent of it carried notes of sweetness. Inappropriate, she felt, for such a somber moment.

Fehln sat quietly beside her as the daystar rose just as silently back into the sky. Its reappearance usually brought relief and celebration, but that morning, the bright rays seemed slightly tempered by the mood.

Elunai looked up as a cardinal settled on a branch not far above her, his crimson feathers flashing wildly in the daybreak. Moments later, his mate joined him, and the pair stared down at the girl in anticipation.

Fehln nodded to them. "Red. Madam."

Mister Red nodded back and chirped, "Bit of an off morning, it seems."

"We lost another one," the albino confirmed, looking back to Elunai. "But at least this one's on her feet already."

Her gaze averted as she moved to stand. "I'll have breakfast out soon. You can let the others know," she said.

Not long after she'd disappeared back into the cottage, an old rabbit emerged from the forest just beyond the apple tree, followed by a small flock of sparrows.

From the other side of the clearing, the faintest sound of aggressive squeaking broke the morning tranquility, gradually growing louder and louder.

"Fehln! You insensitive twit!" fussed a flurry of grey barreling across the meadow.

The albino turned just in time to jump kick the small yet ferocious pair of front teeth flying straight at him. His insufferable counterpart spiraled off to the side on impact. "Idiot," he snapped back. "I'm not babying her anymore."

The other squirrel spat as he got to his feet. "Babying! Empathy! Not the same, cloud puff!" He crouched, readying himself for another launch.

"Hi, Miiskoe," came the muffled, human voice.

The two looked up as Elunai crossed the stone-paved corner of the garden to a large rock, a sack of millet and sunflower seeds in hand and a chunk of cheese lodged between her lips.

The flat-topped boulder leveled at her waist, a natural table amongst the shrubbery lining the property. The apple tree's outermost branches stretched over one end of the slab and hovered a small, A-framed bird feeder just above the surface. A wooden, rodent-sized trough sat on the other end, complete with an obscure, leafy canopy tied to its sides.

Elunai filled both compartments, leaving an extra row of feed scattered between the two. She'd barely tied the bag back up when the swarm of wildlife settled in for their morning meal.

A small smile played at the girl's lips as she stepped away from the breakfast crew, finishing off her cheese. So many big personalities among such small creatures, yet they all seemed to mesh in the presence of food.

8

Morning routines were a blessing. They allowed for the forgetting of a lonely life in an isolated place surrounded by a constant, unseen threat. How bad could it really be when every material need was met on the daily?

After breakfast, the modest array of crop sprouts and flowers were watered and weeded. Firewood was restocked in the cottage from the pile kept in the stable. Floors were swept, and water pitchers were filled from the well pump near the stream.

Following, the meticulous reorganization of the cupboards and shelves had to occur. Multiple layers of them lined the living and kitchen walls of the front room, filled with traded wares, foods, medicines, and other supplies. They never looked right to Elunai. Always too cluttered and busy. Perhaps *that* morning she could finally find a configuration that seemed less...overwhelming? Maybe.

Hours passed. Chaos ensued. The girl successfully reorganized the mess to look...like a slightly different mess.

Biting her lip and breathing back a deep frustration, she closed her eyes and quickly shook her head. "Just don't look at it. This never happened," she told herself.

And with that, she turned on heel.

Then came the upstairs preparations. There was no telling when another traveler would visit the glade, but Elunai eagerly kept the beds ready just in case.

The planks of the staircase creaked under her toes at the lightest steps. She'd tried finding quieter spots along the aged wood, but there weren't many left.

The loft had begun to warm a bit with the season, and there was always a bit of heat radiating from the stone chimney that rose through the far end of the room.

Elunai removed the cape hanging from her shoulders and placed it overtop one of the crates sitting in the corner before moving to push open the small, round window in the left-center wall. From there, she could take in the expanse of the clearing.

The daystar's rays graced every feature in a soft, yet bright warmth. Grasses sparkled as the dew evaporated, and the fauna scurried busily about their own agendas.

The maiden watched as even the littlest creatures fluttered in and out of the forest as though it had no bearing on their safety, despite the horrors they had witnessed time and time again.

Why couldn't she? Why *wouldn't* she?

Mister and Missus Red could be heard debating the location of their spring nest as the maiden pushed away from the window.

That life of hers in the quiet of the glade was secure. She saw no reason to ever abandon it.

Two narrow beds bordered the sides of the chimney with a large nightstand set squarely in between them. Elunai pulled the dust covers from each to shake them out into the fresh air before folding them and placing them in a nearby crate.

"Oh?" Fehln asked as he popped onto the windowsill from the roof. "Expecting company today?"

The girl's ears grew warmer as she shifted focus. She usually replaced those covers on the beds after their dusting. "Maybe...just a feeling." Her hands quickly busied themselves in fluffing pillows.

Fehln watched her with a subtle smile on his chops. A long while had passed since their last visitor, and the anticipation wasn't unwarranted.

"Are you coming in or not? I'm closing this," Elunai said, striding over to the window.

White fluff bounded onto the loft floor and headed for the steps.

Reaching out to pull the window shut, a flash of light from the southern woods stole Elunai's attention.

It was only a second, but the girl knew what she had seen.

Half a minute passed before she let herself breath again. A slow, hesitant breath released as she finally shut the wood-framed glass.

Squeezing her eyes shut, Elunai vigorously patted her cheeks and shook her head, attempting to rid herself of the apprehension that had welled up.

"The apple blossoms will disappear soon..." she whispered to no one, moving back toward the steps.

CHAPTER 3

"How many times have you seen it now?" Fehln asked.

He sat atop the garden rock with two, mis-matched tea cups before him. The one closest to him held his day's-worth of fresh water, and the water in front of Elunai was steeping with blue herbs.

"I don't know...a handful of times," she replied.

"Do you know what it is?"

"I think it's a bird. I've tried to get a closer look, but it always disappears into the forest as soon as I get near. Why does it glow? Why would it keep coming around but never into the meadow?"

"The goldfinch doesn't need to visit here." Fehln slid his muzzle across the surface of his drink.

"You know about this?!"

"In a way. We've all seen him on occasion. I hadn't realized you'd started to. Maybe you should go meet him..."

Elunai's jaw shifted forward and she sat back on her log stool, glaring daggers at the rodent. Never. That risk wasn't worth her safety...and he was pressuring her again.

"Sounds like you haven't learned much about it by venturing out yourself..." she mumbled.

"Calm down. Drink your tea."

"*Felici*-tea," she corrected, bringing the cup to her lips.

Oh, yes. How dare he downplay the bliss that was her self-made, luxury brew experience? The squirrel rolled his eyes.

A mere moment after her first sip, Elunai and Fehln caught the sound of a small, desperate cry on the eastern end of the clearing.

Jumping up, the two of them made for the brook as the little sound grew closer.

Fehln saw it first. He bared his teeth, leaping ahead of the maiden, and readied a strike.

The second chipmunk in the course of a day bounded up to meet the squirrel's challenge and leapt up onto the old tree stump in the field for higher ground.

"Fehln! Wait!" Elunai called.

The clash was inevitable. Unless they were clearly dying, Fehln didn't tolerate strange animals on the premises, crying or not.

A flurry of white and rust tumbled about the field as Fehln apprehended the most imposing nemesis.

"Hey! *Fehln*...!" the girl emphasized, chasing after the blur.

The commotion attracted some of the more Fehln-tolerated creatures to the scene.

Miiskoe cackled hysterically. "Doth mine eyes deceive me, or is Tiny besting Noble Snowflake?" he mocked.

Somehow, *that* voice got through and heightened the albino's ferocity. High-pitched growling erupted from the brawl.

"Don't worry! There was only ever room out here for one of our fat tails!" the grey squirrel called. A pebble suddenly pegged him between the ears, sending his prompt sneer in the direction from which it came. "Remlli?!"

The old rabbit sat quietly beside the trunk of the apple tree. Stoic, though he was, there was no way he wasn't the guilty party, and it didn't take a word to communicate his displeasure with the squirrel's incitement.

Miiskoe's eye twitched as he turned away and mumbled something about a decrepit varmint.

In a last ditch effort to quell the epic Spat of Rodents, Elunai threw her cape over the struggling pile of fur.

A spooked chipmunk darted out from under the fabric and climbed back up into a hollow on the tree stump.

Fehln cursed under his breath as he emerged a moment later. "Really...?" he asked, looking up at the girl.

She shot him an unamused glance. "You're missing large tufts off your back and still questioning me?" Elunai turned to head for the stump. "I just want to talk to this one."

The chipmunk visibly trembled, paced the hollow, and stared the girl down.

Elunai put up her hands as she approached, her voice gently assuring, "You're safe."

"Don't...!" the little one chirped, unsure of how to handle the larger being... who could apparently speak with him.

"I promise...you're safe," Elunai repeated as her movements ceased. "I just want to know who you are. I've never seen you around."

The breaths of the small creature gradually began to slow, as did his pacing. Tiny, slender paws wrung about themselves as the chipmunk considered his response.

"Uhm..." he started. "Pikan."

"That's your name?"

"Yea'."

"Ah...welcome to the haven, Pikan. I'm Elunai. I live here with Fehln and the others." The girl gestured to those gathered across the clearing.

Pikan glanced in the direction she indicated for only a split second, his trust still lacking.

"So, what's going on? Was there something in the woods?" she asked.

The chipmunk shook his head, his eyes fading into a glassy, forlorn state.

Fehln sauntered up next to Elunai, scratching some extra loose fur off his neck. "If you need an interrogator..." he started.

"Stop..." the girl muttered.

"Have you...seen my mate?" came the timid voice from the hollow. "She went out to gather food yesterday evenin'...and she didn't come back to the den."

At that, both Elunai and her albino companion fell silent.

Copper-blonde bangs slid over the bridge of her nose as the maiden lowered her head in tandem with a sinking heart.

Fehln glanced over to the freshly-packed patch of dirt beneath the apple tree. Delicate, white petals had already fallen over top of it, blending the grave ever more slightly into the earth. Suddenly, he looked back up and his ears snapped to attention. "Elunai..."

The urgency in his voice forced her gaze up as well.

The movement in the eastern woods was faint, but it was there. The sound of crunching gravel soon followed suit.

"Fehln," Elunai breathed, "please, take Pikan to the garden and explain..."

The squirrel shot her a heavy grimace. That was certainly one way out of a hard conversation.

Before Fehln could protest, Elunai ran for the cottage. Bursting through the front door, the maiden snatched the wooden staff leaning against the wall just off to the left. Her ears rung with the sounds from the forest growing nearer...and that of her own heartbeat.

Gripping the staff tightly, she stepped back out onto the front steps, crouched low behind the thick ivy covering the side of the house, and kept her line of sight glued in the direction of footbridge.

She finally caught sight of a large, shadowed figure approaching the stream - quiet, save for the sound of its footfalls on the earth and...humming?

Only a moment of that familiar tune and Elunai jumped back up, set her staff against the door frame, and rattled the old steps in her haste out to the path.

The figure stepped out from under the thick shade of the trees and onto the log bridge. There, the sizable mountain man paused to take in the sweet air amidst the daystar rays. He switched his walking stick to his left hand to stroke the long, ashen beard flowing from his face to his chest with his right.

"Mister Keamotus!" he heard a feminine voice call. Readjusting his vision to the bright clearing, the man beheld a flash of copper and blonde rushing toward him just before Elunai jumped.

The impact and a giant step back caused a noisy ruckus of clanking cookware and tools as they swayed about his towering travel pack.

"Oho...!" he chuckled in amusement. "That looks like Elunai!"

"It's me," she beamed into her hug.

"You'll have to forgive me, my eyes are still adjusting from that trek through the woods."

Her smile fell a bit as she resisted glancing at the menacing trees behind him.

The man raised up his bicep parallel to the bridge. "I can still carry a swinging pumpkin head, though!"

Elunai snickered. "I believe you! But maybe you should rest first...?"

"Aye...that's a good idea."

"Come on in! I'll get you some water and you can tell me about your trip."

The traveler moved to follow Elunai as she headed back for the cottage. "That's fine, thank you as always. I'll only be a few hours, though. No need to put up with my snoring overnight."

Elunai stopped short. "What...?"

Keamotus waved his hand in light gesture. "Honestly, it's alright. This one's a longer journey and I need to make headway."

The girl turned again, hiding the sudden disappointment in her eyes. "I see..."

Once indoors, Keamotus unloaded his bag onto the kitchen floor and sat heavily upon one of the table benches with an equally weighty sigh.

"Sometimes...I wonder how much longer these legs of mine are going to keep this up," he mused.

As Elunai procured the largest clay drinking cup she owned, the man caught sight of the glimmering star brooch on her mantle.

"Looks like it's gone dim. Why don't you wear it?" he asked.

The girl was silent for a moment as she watched the clear stream of liquid pour from its pitcher. "I like looking at it near the fire. Feels like it shines more there," she answered.

He could hear the bitterness through that

innocent tone. Keamotus made sure to catch Elunai's gaze with his as she handed him the cup. "The Stelluvak Star is meant to be worn, young lady..." he told her. "I think you're aware of the way it resonates with a soul."

"Yeah," the girl said. "If the wearer bears light."

After a long, quenching drink, the man sighed again. "Oh, child..." he said. Without another word, Keamotus set his cup down on the table and began rustling through his pack.

Elunai watched as he pulled out various items and placed them next to the empty cup in a frustratingly slow manner. The girl's hands clasped tightly as anticipation swept through in a heated wave. After a few lengthy moments, her patience was rewarded as a sizable loaf of bread finally came into view.

"Indeed, I thought you might," he smiled, motioning for her to come forward. When she drew near, he placed the loaf in her two outstretched hands. "Better eat that up quick. Likely won't keep long in these warmer temperatures," he said.

The smile returned to her face. "Thank you...! I think it should actually do pretty well in the cellar if I pack it right." She hadn't been graced with the heavenly taste of bread since the last time he'd visited.

He stopped her from turning to the kitchen counter, "Hold on - a couple more things." He stacked a small, wooden container atop the bread in her hands and an even smaller fabric sack on top of that.

"What is it?" she asked.

"Go on, you'll see."

Balancing the items across the kitchen, Elunai carefully set each of them down on the counter before prying the box open. "Oh, salt!" she exclaimed.

"And under it...?"

Grabbing a spoon, Elunai started scraping away at the surface grains. Layer by layer, small cubes of fresh, northern salmon began to appear, and the girl's jaw dropped lower and lower. She glanced over her shoulder at Keamotus with a childish grin plastered clear across her face.

"Mmmhm," he nodded. Her quiet enthusiasm was thanks enough.

"Just going to...hide this from Fehln," Elunai whispered to herself as she covered the fish back up. That was one meal she didn't intend on sharing.

The bag he had given her contained another assortment of tea leaves, which she gleefully added to her collection in the cupboard. How did that man always seem to find the most exquisite gifts?

"Where did your travels take you this past season?" she asked, turning back to him. "Other than north."

"Oh...maybe a little to the northeast." The man's beard twitched a bit, signaling how hard he was fighting a smile.

Elunai's expression immediately gave way to annoyance. He knew...he *knew* how those vague responses tore at her insides.

"Well now...I'd best go down for a nap if I'm going to have the strength to continue on later. May I borrow one of the loft beds?" the man asked.

"Always," Elunai replied, "but I have to ask...why is your journey so pressing this time? Even when you've had a long way to go, you have always stayed at least a day or two. Is something wrong?"

Keamotus rose from his seat and brushed a few stubborn folds from his old tunic. "There are places to be, my dear...things to do," he said with a wink.

"Please," she begged. "If you can't stay, at least tell me something about the world out there. *Anything.*"

His expression turned soft then, taking in the desperation she used to keep hidden in seasons gone by. Keamotus reached out and pulled the girl into a proper hug, which she eagerly returned. "Elunai," he said, "I know you're lonely here, and I don't want that for you - I deeply wish things were different. But I will tell you now what I've always told you." He pulled away just enough to look her in the eyes.

"Yeah," she said in a heavy tone, "be change to get change...and if I want to know...I have to find out." Elunai stepped away from him completely, looking utterly betrayed. "Let me get your canteen. I'll fill it before you leave."

As her guest rested, Elunai headed back out into the garden to face the impending, gut-wrenching music. There, she found Fehln and Pikan sitting quietly under the apple tree. She stopped a few feet away, waiting for Fehln's rebuke. But it never came.

Pikan's form bent low as he silently grieved over his mate's burial site with a sorrow that seemed too heavy for his tiny soul to bear.

Elunai's index finger twitched forward and her arm began to reach out, a powerful desire to comfort him washing over her. She stopped at Fehln's glance and a shake of his head.

Time was the necessary companion in that moment.

The girl lowered to a crouch and hugged her knees, not taking her eyes off the bereft forest dweller. "Pikan...I'm sorry..." she started quietly, "You're welcome to stay here in the glade if you'd like." Again, she deftly ignored a scowl from Fehln. "And I promise...I'll find a way to save them...all those like your mate...someday."

Without waiting for a response, the maiden rose and headed off to distract herself with additional chores.

Fehln watched as she headed back into the cottage and reemerged with a basket of laundry and her washboard. He sighed. "I'd better go with her. She doesn't do well near the trees."

"I don't blame 'er," Pikan voiced quietly.

For the first time since the chipmunk entered the glade, Fehln left him alone. Pikan turned as his would-be nemesis sauntered off to accompany the maiden on her daring linen quest and wondered about the strange dynamic unfolding there in the haven. A human girl who could speak with animals, a squirrel who felt the need to watch after her, and the inexplicable reason Pikan's mate sought refuge there after years of living in the woods.

"You ever wonder if you poison the fish when you do that?" Fehln asked.

Elunai didn't look up as she continued running a garment over the ridges of her board. "It's just a little soap I got from one of the traveler's from the east. I like how it smells."

"But do you know what it *tastes* like?" he goaded.

She fully realized he was doing that to keep her mind off the unnatural darkness on the other side of the brook, but great daystar did it get under her skin. "You ever wonder if you poison *me* when you do that?"

"Nope."

The girl glanced over and found the squirrel staring intently into the trees before them. "What is it...?"

"Nothing," he replied quickly. "But your little sympathy case is staring."

"My wha-" Elunai looked around for a moment before laying eyes on Pikan, perched on the tree stump just inside the old corral fence. His little hand-like paws suddenly rose to rub at his muzzle. "Hm..." she breathed, turning back to her work. "I wonder how he feels about this place."

"Let's ask."

"No-"

"Hey, Tiny! Join us or leave us, but don't stare, it's rude."

Elunai's hands plopped into the water with a sound splash as her eyes rolled. "Why are you like this..."

To both of their surprise, Pikan slowly made his way over to the bank and sat himself down on the opposite side of Elunai from Fehln.

Wringing out her newly cleaned tunic, the girl laid it out over the edge of her basket and pulled the next garment out. She felt if she kept busy, she wouldn't have to strike up any awkward or imposing conversation with the newcomer.

"Your hands are shakin'," Pikan noted.

Well, so much for that.

"Of course - she just realized she's poisoning fish," Fehln said.

Pikan leaned forward to peer worriedly out into the water, then up at Fehln. "What?"

The squirrel managed the most masterful expression then, communicating to the chipmunk that he didn't want to offend right after the death of Pikan's mate...but that the smaller creature was being incredibly dense.

"So, um..." Elunai spoke, feeling as though she had no other choice, "Have you ever seen the goldfinch?"

Pikan looked back up to her, noticing she was working twice as intently to finish the laundry. "I have. He's been coming 'round a lot more lately."

"Have you ever met him? Talked to him?"

"Well, no...he tends to keep to 'imself."

Elunai's shoulders visibly slumped. "I just want to know more about him. I feel like...I mean...why is he so bright...?" her voice trailed off.

"I heard a rumor that he might've come from the daystar. That could be just speculation, though. You...could go see 'im for yourself?" Pikan suggested. "Bein' that you can talk to us 'n' all."

Fehln hid a smirk. "Now *there's* an idea..." he murmured before taking a sudden wall of water to the face.

CHAPTER 4

Evening arrived, once again, all too quickly.

Keamotus situated the travel pack where it belonged on his back and unhurriedly strode out the front door.

Elunai followed him with Fehln on her shoulder and torch alight. "Are you sure you're okay to go out there during the night...?" she asked.

"I've done this many times, dear one. Got plenty of light," he replied in that gentle, yet hardy voice of his. "Oh, by the way, I left a package on the table upstairs. Just something to help you through the coming summer months."

Elunai bowed her head and managed a smile. "Why are you so kind to me?"

Keamotus let out a low chuckle. "Oh, I think you should take that up with the person who gave you that brooch."

Elunai's head tilted in curiosity.

"Something tells me they care for you just the same...but that you'd heed their word a bit over mine."

The maiden was taken aback. "That's...not true," she said. "Why would you think that?"

Keamotus paused a moment to look at her in sincerity. "Are you aware of why she gave that to you?"

Elunai slightly nodded. "The...light she thought I could wield."

"And you know where that light comes from?"

The girl averted her gaze. "A certain kind of...spirit. That some people have. Not everyone." The toe of her boot dug half circles into the dirt beneath it as she resisted looking him in the eye.

The man pressed his lips together and arched his eyebrows, a sound 'hm' rumbling through his throat as he turned to head down the pathway again.

Elunai's face flushed slightly and she could feel Fehln's albino eyes roll back in that little head of his.

As they reached the southern border of the clearing, the daystar was just melting beyond the tree line.

Infinitely more at ease with her capable human friend on the path with her, Elunai swiftly lit the large lanterns at the edge of the forest. True, she would have to face the eastern set with only Fehln, but at least the battle was half over.

"Beautiful..." Keamotus whispered, placing a hand on one of the lampposts. "I do wish there could be light like this everywhere. So..." He turned back to Elunai. "Have you given any more thought to venturing out to new places?"

"Have you given any more thought to telling me what places there are to venture to?" She regretted the sharp question as soon as she asked it. "No..." she said. "I'm pretty sure I belong here."

The man took in a deep breath and sighed. His eyes held a semblance of what looked like sadness, but he nodded his head.

"It's a beautiful place...this haven of yours. I hope someday I'll get to see you grow."

Elunai nodded, unsure of exactly what to make of that. Before she registered the shift, Mister Keamotus was off again, humming down the dirt road into darkness, and she couldn't help but notice he never carried a lantern.

～ .⊹ ✧ ⊹. ～

Savory scents of seasoned, salmon stew wafted through the cottage that night as Elunai made use of the traveler's more perishable gift. She was grateful Fehln had chosen to sleep outside that evening - made keeping her dinner a secret much easier.

She sat at the edge of the hearth, stirring the contents of the large pot with one hand, while turning over the fabric of her new sundress in the other. She wondered at how Keamotus knew exactly what size to get her despite how long it had been since their last meeting. The light blue and yellow gift would fit perfectly.

"Am I still growing...?" she wondered aloud.

Come to think of it, she wasn't entirely sure she had physically matured at all over the last few years. At least nothing new seemed to come of her shape, or her reflection in the mirror. Was it supposed to?

Bringing the ladle to her mouth, Elunai blew gently on the steaming chunks of vegetables and fish before sampling her new concoction. She stifled a laugh as she swallowed and licked her lips. "Well, there's plenty of salt in there." Grabbing a thick cloth, Elunai lifted the pot off the spit and set it next to her on the hearth. "Good enough." She rose and turned to the cupboards for a bowl.

Just as she stepped away from the fireplace, her peripheral sight caught a shadow move outside the large living room window. Spinning to face it, her feet instinctively took her further from the glass.

Silence. Stillness.

After a moment, she realized the shadow was still there, outside, barely moving at the base of the floor-to-ceiling frame.

In an instant, her staff was back in her grasp as Elunai forced herself to step closer. "...Fehln?" she asked. But it couldn't have been him - it was too big.

At no response, she moved even closer to the window, staff pointed in defense despite the glass that separated her from the outside. The shadow was definitely *much* larger than Fehln. But then, she noticed the very distinct outline of a fuzzy plump of fur.

The staff lowered and Elunai shifted to her knees, crawling cautiously to investigate further.

Finally, she saw it, and her lips parted in astonishment.

There, staring intently at the firelight through her window, was a large, lone raccoon. Somehow, it didn't seem to see her very well as it bobbed its head around trying to make sense of what was going on beyond the intricate, wooden window frame.

"Another new visitor..." Elunai whispered against the glass. "Where did you come from?"

The coon suddenly looked up and realized she was kneeling there. Startled, it backed away and slid off the stone ledge it had been sitting on. "Oh, wait...!" Elunai called.

She lifted off the floor and ran to the door. Releasing the lock and

stepping into the chilled, spring air, the girl just barely caught the masked beast waddling silently off into the night.

"Oh..." she breathed again. "I'm really sorry. Please, stay safe out there." Her hand laced through the hair against her head.

Making a mental note to leave a handful nuts on the window ledge the next evening, Elunai slipped back indoors to finish her meal. Her mind spun with reasons for all the new acquaintances she was making those days.

What was bringing them to the glade?

CHAPTER 5

Before long, as Elunai had forecasted, the remainder of her beloved apple blossoms met with the earth to make way for the fullness of summer leaves.

The garlic and corn were well on their way to maturity while the rest of the garden had already burst into full swing. The cosmos and sunflowers would take a bit longer to grow, but their appearance brought the sensation of life and warmth Elunai craved. The brook seemed to swell with vigor in kind as newly spawned rainbow trout started on their journey.

Blue and yellow pastel hung lightly from Elunai's shoulders as she sat on the bank in her new summer dress with Fehln on her right and Pikan on her left. Daystar rays caught the copper in her hair and brought out a red that rivaled the brightness of her blonde ends.

The simple, wooden fishing pole in her hand didn't seem to tremble quite as much that day. Perhaps it had something to do with the surrounding abundance of goodness that seemed to visibly push back on the darkness of the woods beyond.

"So, how does it feel?" Fehln asked.

The maiden slightly leaned in his direction with a curious expression. "Fishing...?"

"No, the dress. Does it fit right?"

"Mhmm..." Elunai let a smile through. She leaned back a ways so that the tails of the halter bow slid off the skin of her shoulder blades. "I especially like how it ties around the back of my neck. I don't think I've seen a style quite like this before! I wonder where he got it..."

"Flows like the stream," Pikan noted as he gnawed on a seed from his stash.

Elunai flared the hem of her skirt with her free hand. "I guess so. I just like how free it makes me feel." She leaned forward again to rest her chest against her raised knees.

A bit of impatience had begun to set in. They'd been out there for at least half an hour with zero catches, and the girl had hoped to enjoy an hour or so of felici-tea and journaling before the evening came. The chances of that were fading.

"Fehln...do you really think I poisoned all the fish with the laundry...?" she asked.

The squirrel was silent, drawing the girl's gaze from the water. He was doing it again...staring intently into the forest.

Elunai knew that meant she shouldn't look. But how could she not? A quick glance over at the chipmunk revealed that he was doing the same. Both rodents were stalk still and visibly tense with ears raised on alert.

The trembling in the maiden's hands returned as she pulled the fishing line out of the stream. Clasping the hook against the rod, Elunai slowly moved the wooden pole to a diagonal position against her body, largely in defense of whatever might be out there. Her line of sight found Fehln again. She wished so ardently to ask if they should leave, but the words wouldn't form in her throat.

Neither companion spoke. There was definitely something out there. Strange that it dared to appear so close to the glade in the middle of the day. Even stranger were the thoughts going through the girl's mind on how the brook could still babble as though nothing was wrong. Couldn't it just...silence itself?

Finally, Elunai's restraint broke, and she glanced into the woods.

A shining pair of eyes met hers from low in the shrouded thicket.

The chill in her blood ran its course.

It was then she noticed that the form seemed solid, contrasting the horrors she'd suffered from before, and her vision wasn't blurring.

Somehow, that gave her the smallest bit of courage for words. "Mister... Coon...?" she inquired.

The mysterious, large raccoon she'd encountered earlier in the spring had begun regular, nightly visits to the glade. The handful of tree nuts she left out in the evenings encouraged the ritual. However, it never let her near enough for a proper greeting and definitely never showed up while the daystar rays still shone.

There was no response from the gleaming set of eyes...not even a blink.

That's when Fehln whispered, "This isn't your concern. It's ours." By 'ours' he surely meant him and Pikan.

"What...?"

"It's a cat."

A full twenty seconds elapsed before Elunai processed what he'd told her, and then her lips mouthed an exaggerated curse.

Lowering the rod, Elunai slowly dipped the line back into the stream, resolving to not let the obscure appearance of yet another new creature get the better of her. Especially not a cat. It *was* a cat...right? He wasn't just saying that to make her feel better...?

Unexpectedly quickly, the fishing line pulled taught. Apparently, those trout preferred their captors on the cusp of a heart attack.

As Elunai pulled back to reel, the eyes across the way began to rise. Occupied though she was, she watched intently with her companions as the dark form slowly grew and grew...and grew in size.

Fehln and Pikan backed away from the bank slightly, sending additional questions through Elunai's mind.

As the figure stepped from the shadows, it retained the dark hue from which it came and was far larger than Fehln had let on.

The trio on the other side of the stream froze.

Feline, yes. But *cat*?!

A fat, hooked trout at the end of Elunai's raised line smacked against the girl's cheek, but she dared not move. The creature was staring straight at her.

Or rather...

No, it was staring at the fish!

Elunai's free hand came up to stop the trout from swaying on the cord.

In turn, the sharp, yellow eyes across the way narrowed.

Moving slowly as to not alarm the visitor, Elunai unhooked her catch. "You... want this?" she asked.

At that, a massive, pink tongue slipped over the equally large, dark chops about the carnivore's muzzle.

The girl barely nodded, drew her hand back, worked up the arm muscles as taut as she could muster, and flung the fish clear to the opposite bank.

Not missing a beat, the creature snatched up the gifted meal and at once bounded back through the shade of the forest.

The companions listened intently as sounds of the giant's retreat grew fainter.

As her breath recovered, Elunai lowered her line, once again, into the brook. Her jaw shifted as she inwardly debated how to address the white fluff on her right.

To her annoyance, he spoke first," Well, that was clo-"

"*Panther.*"

"Eh?"

"Not a cat...*panther.*"

"Same thing."

"Wh...!" Elunai turned to Pikan who was finally re-settling next to his seed pile. "Pikan, tell me you understand the difference between the big felines and the little ones."

Pikan side-glanced with cheeks very intentionally stuffed to the brim. His little paws came up to his muzzle again and began vigorously rubbing until the girl threw her free hand up in frustration.

"There are no 'little' felines," Fehln said. "Just death with a meow."

Elunai sunk deeper into the grassy bank beneath her, thoroughly giving up on the matter. "Why did it visit anyway? Where are all these new animals coming from? I never thought I'd see something like *that* out here."

Fehln had undoubtedly noticed the uptick as each new encounter seemed to upset him, but he never spoke at length about any of it.

With cheeks only slightly cleared and voice muffled, Pikan said, "Well...I can't speak for the others...but when I came lookin' for my mate, somethin' guided me to this glade. Maybe the same happened for her...is what I think."

"Something?" Elunai questioned.

"Don't know...it was warm, invitin'..."

"The daystar?"

"I don't think so. This may sound strange, but...it was somethin' I felt and didn't see. And I still feel it every day I'm here. I like it."

"Well, that's how I feel about the daystar," Elunai sighed. "Anyway...I just want my lunch...and my tea."

"*Felici*-tea," the albino corrected. He nearly ended up on that hook himself.

The light tap of delicate clay pieces coming together broke the afternoon silence across the cottage as Elunai re-sealed the lid of a nearly empty counter pot. Dusting remnants of pecan off her hands, she made her way to the open entryway.

"Fehln," she called, "we're running low on tree nuts."

The squirrel looked up from his seat next to Pikan on the old tree stump, and the girl bit back a smile. She couldn't betray her thorough approval of their unlikely, yet growing companionship in front of him.

"Alright, I'll get Miiskoe for this run," Fehln said.

"Would you two...survive each other out there?" Pikan asked, having become acutely aware of the rivalry in the squirrel circle.

"I'll beat him into submission..." Fehln grunted. He quickly retrieved the handkerchief 'sack' from Elunai.

As Fehln hopped out to the woods in search of his grey counterpart, the maiden took up his previous spot next to Pikan. The two of them sat in silence for a long moment, watching Fehln disappear from sight.

Then, Pikan sensed the rigidity well up through Elunai's form. "They'll be a'ight," he told her.

She sucked in a breath. "What's it like...? The wooded world..."

"He hasn't told you?"

"Just...from your perspective..."

Pikan grew quiet again as he stared out into the shrouded thicket, sorting through his thoughts. His petite, yet striking, dark eyes shimmered in the daystar's rays, and the sight of such a small creature contemplating so deeply gave the young woman pause.

"I haven't actually seen most of it," he started, "but there're countless paths that cross through those trees. Some are wide 'n' well traveled while some are so small, only those my size 'n' smaller could fit through 'em."

"Where do they lead? Is it dark all the way through?" Elunai had fully turned to face the chipmunk, her eyes filled with an intense curiosity.

"I didn't live far from here - there's enough light from the daystar to see at least a few hops ahead...usually. An' there are some smaller clearings I've scavenged. But I couldn't say where each path leads. Too far for my kind to travel. Although, there are rumors..."

"Rumors? What kind? Have you talked to anyone who's been out there?" Elunai leaned in a touch closer with every question.

Pikan turned back to her, an amused smile playing at his tiny features. "Well... I've lived in the woods all my life...reaped its offerings an', so far, evaded its curse. But my mate and I kept largely to ourselves 'n' had no need or desire to venture very far."

Elunai sank back with an audible exhale. "Well, why did you choose to live out there when it's so dangerous?"

"It's just the way o' things. Ya learn to live it. I really couldn't imagine life without the wooded world."

Life without the wooded world...

Viridescent irises began to glaze as Elunai's focus dared to creep toward the forest's edge.

What would *that* be like?

"There was a skunk I passed one day on his way out on the main road east. He disappeared for months 'n' when we saw him again, he'd multiplied!"

"Excuse me...?" The horrified expression didn't match the restraint in Elunai's voice.

A snicker-squeak escaped the chipmunk's throat. "Well, wherever he went, he found a mate."

The slow roll of her eyes brought the forest back into view before the girl turned to hug her knees up to her chin in defeat.

"Elunai...bein' honest, I've never met anyone so curious who didn't want to explore."

The maiden's chin sunk deeper between her knees. "I do want to..."

"Then why-"

"I can't."

He caught the waiver in her voice and fell back into silence.

The candid confessions were becoming more frequent, and with them, the apparent sting of desperation.

Sounds of a nearing ruckus from the direction of the apple tree released the pair from their brief, yet uncomfortable standstill.

Elunai stood, quite ready to retrieve her fresh haul of tree nuts. Yet, as she looked up, the sight of squirrels was not what greeted her gaze.

Three sparrows from the breakfast crew flailed frantically under the apple tree's branches, one on the ground, two fluttering just above it.

Instinct launched Elunai into a full sprint toward the flock, Pikan on her heels.

"What's wrong?!" she asked, dropping to the earth beside the grounded bird.

"There was an encounter in the woods...! We didn't see it, we were just flying through some branches!" one of the airborne sparrows chirped.

"We heard a strange noise and then she just started falling," explained the other.

Elunai felt the ice begin to creep through her chest.

No, no, no, no...

Mind racing, Elunai shuffled through the familiar motion of gently cradling a small creature in the hem of her garment and rushing it through the open cottage doorway. Once again, she found herself atop the plush rug of that front room, leaning over the pages of her guidebook, praying...haunted.

The girl could feel Pikan's presence behind her, his anticipatory gaze fixed on the situation...on her. She had made him a promise that she'd never forget. In a way, she'd made it largely to herself.

"I don't understand..." she breathed, "there are no wounds on this one either, yet..."

Late afternoon rays poured through the large, fireside window and embraced each form in the room. At their subtle warmth, Elunai's breathing gradually deepened even as the struggling sparrow's life force began to subside.

The two other birds hopped anxiously around the girl bent over their friend, trying to leave space while struggling to contain their distress.

"Stay with me...I've got you..." Elunai whispered as she lowered her head further over the dying animal. Her whole body became a shelter from all but the beams of light. "You're safe. You're not alone."

Pikan tilted his head. The sudden gleam of the Stelluvak Star brooch hanging on the mantle caught his attention for just a moment, and then his small ears picked up the even smaller sound of tears hitting the floor.

The young woman's back hitched, fingers tucking into fists.

In a flurry of motion, the guidebook went sailing across the room, crashing into the kitchen table before hitting the floor in a wrinkled mess of pages.

Starved for breath and with hot regret streaming down her cheeks, Elunai recoiled from the throw, gently collected the deceased vessel, and pushed herself to her feet. Catching sight of the three there with her, she tried to speak...to apologize...to beg for forgiveness. The sound stopped cold in her throat as the visible agony tearing through their little forms decimated what remained of her resolve.

Elunai's gaze intersected Pikan's. Her eyes quickly expressed everything her voice couldn't before she forced herself back out into the clearing, chest ablaze with the pangs of guilt.

The muffled fussing of two, familiar rodents wafted over the evening air through stuffed mouths and gritted teeth.

"Stop *dragging* it...!"

"I've got the heavier end, you pallid mutant!"

It took everything Fehln had in him to not drop his side of the sack and roundhouse those foul incisors into the next season. Perhaps asking Pikan to help with the gathering would've been the better idea - despite how the chipmunk's size would undoubtedly caused the pouch to drag anyway.

"At least get in step with me so we don't-" The fabric suddenly fell from Fehln's teeth.

Miiskoe watched in horror as all the freshly-picked tree nuts spilled out onto the dirt just as they reached the apple tree. "You did not..."

The grey squirrel didn't even have time to pounce. Fehln took off running across the darkening meadow.

"Yo!" As Miiskoe regarded Fehln's retreat, he caught sight of the abnormality responsible for his counterpart's strange behavior.

There was Elunai...lighting the border lamps...all on her own.

"Elunai! Are you okay?" Fehln asked as he approached her, "You don't have to do this alone...why didn't you wait?"

The left lantern at the southern entrance took its flame, and Elunai swung her torch toward the next, her expression chiseled in numb despondence.

"Hey...!" the squirrel tried again. He looked on in utter bewilderment as the girl carried on in complete silence, not so much as flinching or sparing him a glance.

Soon enough, the second lantern was lit, and Elunai turned to head east.

Fehln followed intently with continued attempts to break through the invisible wall keeping her unresponsive. He'd never seen her in such a state.

Reaching the footbridge, Elunai halted in between the two lampposts and stared straight out into the woods. Then, in a surreal display of either courage or complete stupidity, the young woman lowered the torch, stepped out onto the bridge and flung a shrill rebuke out into the expanding darkness.

Fehln froze.

As if in response, the shadows stirred unnaturally against the fading daystar until they consumed every branch untouched by the light. The trees, even full of leaves, looked completely dead.

The two at the forest's edge suddenly felt the tension deep in their bones. The innate sense of despair. The utter loss of any semblance of safety. No words, no sounds, just threat.

The squirrel lunged forward. He didn't know if he'd have to bite or body slam the girl to get her to move, but he had to do something.

Just before he reached her, Elunai spun and forced her flame across the two readied wicks with such abandon that Fehln wondered if he was beholding same human.

A burst of light sprung forth to meet the shadow lashing at Elunai's turned back. A deep hiss reverberated through the thicket, and Elunai glanced toward it just as a retreating, smoke-like tendril sliced across a familiar, white blur.

Her stoic expression at last gave way to sheer horror.

CHAPTER 6

That night was the longest of her life.

She hadn't even bothered to take Fehln indoors. Miiskoe, Pikan, and the mourning sparrows joined Elunai by the garden fire pit as the girl tended the dark wound at the base of the albino's tail.

There was no blood - just a pitch-black gash where white fur once settled. A sense of dread set in with the symptoms the squirrel was experiencing.

Elunai wasn't certain if washing and dressing the lesion would help, but it's all she knew to do in the moment. Silent prayers slipped through moving lips as she worked even though she hardly believed in their power any longer.

What sustained the feeling of ice in her limbs was the way Fehln was struggling to stay conscious. The gash seemed merely a flesh wound...but his small body was responding as though it had been crushed. He could barely move or speak, but he tried...

"Hang in there..." he forced through a raspy throat.

At that, Elunai could no longer hold the tears at bay for the second time that evening. Why was it all happening? Why Fehln? The death-bent blade ripping through her core finally registered as insatiable shame and guilt over everything she was and had done.

"Aw, come on...that's a stubborn rear end right there - a cut won't best it. Might leave a scar...keep him humble," Miiskoe asserted. His intent aside, the delivery didn't seem to faze Elunai in the slightest.

"You weren't supposed to do that," she shot at Fehln.

Fehln mustered an amused grunt, shifting his head atop the makeshift pillow of apple leaves. "As if you could've taken that attack."

She turned to look him square in those weary, little eyes. "I wanted to."

A still silence befell the souls present, and the crackling of the fire pit suddenly seemed a powerful sting in each of their ears.

Pikan moved slowly into the maiden's unwavering line of sight. "What...?" he asked.

After another moment, she shook her head, the quiet tears resuming. Her body bent over Fehln and her hands rested lightly about her friend's frail form. She could hear his labored breath uncomfortably well at that level, and it sent sickening pangs through her gut. "Please..."

One of the sparrows suddenly perked up at a stirring movement over the darkened field. He nudged the feathered companion next to him. "Lei...do you see that?" he whispered.

Sure enough, there was a figure making its way into the clearing from the eastern bridge.

"Elunai...!" Pikan whispered.

In a flurry of motion, the able-bodied creatures scurried for the shelter of nearby bushes as Elunai tensed in place. Even if she'd tried to move Fehln at that point, there was nowhere to run or hide from a threat already on the premises.

She kept her eyes in the direction of the shadow while simultaneously searching for anything she could use as a weapon. Reaching for a loose stone by the fire, she heard a human voice.

"So, this is where all the fireflies gather," the man said. What a strangely chipper tone for such a late, foreign encounter.

Elunai's fingers closed over the rock as she pulled it closer to where she was sitting, suddenly noticing that there were, in fact, fireflies gracing the meadow like hundreds of tiny daystars.

"Who are you?" she asked, still unable to see him clearly. Another who didn't carry a lantern through the forest.

"My name is Jikyshu," he responded. His features finally illuminated in the firelight. He was a younger, more slender man than Mister Keamotus with dark hair and smiling eyes that matched in color.

Elunai wondered how he could possibly be so jovial-looking after having just emerged from the woods at night.

"Forgive my late intrusion. I've heard a great deal about this fabled Daystar Haven. The forest is unusually restless this evening. I thought it best to seek a safer place to set up camp until it settles," Jikyshu explained.

Elunai wasn't sure how to respond as countless thoughts vied for space in her mind. Tales of the meadow? A stranger wanted stay the night. That wasn't the time, Fehln was in trouble. The whole forest was upset...with *her*?

The man continued, "Of course...I'd also heard about the customary trade for shelter. I've brought tribute, should you allow me to stay. Even brought my own tent."

Indeed, he carried a substantial pack on his back, similar to the other travelers she'd met.

"Uhm..." she started.

"Is that a squirrel?"

Elunai sucked in a sharp breath as Jikyshu noticed Fehln. She looked down at her companion still hanging on for his life and felt the wave of overwhelm crash back over her. "I...need to find a way to save him."

The state of Fehln's tail along with the sudden, honest vulnerability in Elunai's voice painted the broader picture for the visitor. Removing the rucksack from his shoulders, Jikyshu set it down against the garden patio with a heavy thud before rummaging through the various compartments.

Elunai grew as curious as she was cautious. With one hand hovering over Fehln in protection, she strained to see what it was the traveler was hunting for.

He produced both a small, rounded tea cup and a vial of dark liquid with glowing flecks of bright aqua intermixed. Popping the cork off of the vial with his teeth, Jikyshu poured the slightest bit of luminescent substance into the cup and held it out to Elunai. "Here, this might help."

She didn't move. "What is that?"

Replacing the cork in its glass, the traveler swirled the vial around to make the liquid glow even brighter. "It's a tonic

made from a plant found in my homeland. The leaves absorb light from the daystar in a way that makes them release excess energy at night in a glow. The extract was found to carry healing properties, specifically for injuries incurred by the darkness."

"You can't be serious..."

The power of light was no mystery, but of all the travelers who'd come through her humble glade, none had even so much as mentioned such a remedy to the forest's curse.

"One way to find out," the man smiled, "And here...just so you know it's safe..." He upturned the cup over his mouth to let a trickle fall over his tongue. Swallowing it back, he moved closer to Elunai to offer her the medicine once again. "It's alright for animals, too. Promise. Or I let you throw me to the shadows."

What choice did she have?

At the increased rate of Fehln's struggling breaths, Elunai reached for the cup, which Jikyshu placed in her hand.

"Hey..." she said softly, turning to the weary creature at her side. "Can you drink?"

Fehln attempted a reply, but could only manage exhausted gasps.

"Okay, don't move, I'll help." Scooping her free hand under his head and neck, Elunai tilted Fehln up ever so slightly and brought the rim of the cup down to his mouth.

Her silent prayers resurfaced as the strange substance was slowly consumed. Elunai briefly glanced back over at the man sitting on the other side of the fire. He was watching Fehln, and his expression bore no signs of deceit. Still...she prayed and waited.

Laying her friend back against the leaves, the girl's hand swept over his back in an impulsive display of care. She knew, if he lived through his ordeal, he'd probably come at her with a curse of his own. Petting, for some reason, had always been the unforgivable sin. But if he didn't make it...

"How long before it takes effect?" Elunai asked.

"For one that small? I'd say...probably about now," Jikyshu smiled.

Her eyes ran back over Fehln's form in a hurry, looking for any signs of change.

First, it was the breath. A once raspy sound began to soften. Fehln drew

a deep inhale as his lungs seemed to free, and then closed his eyes on a tired, yet smooth-sounding sigh.

"You okay...?" Elunai asked. Her hand came up to check on him, but before she could touch him, she noticed a shift in his tail's appearance. She could no longer see the black gash under the thin bandaging and turned back to Jikyshu. "The wounds...do they just..."

"If it's no longer dark, that means the light did its work," the man replied. "I'd keep those wrappings on for a while, though."

"Fehln...!" the girl cried in relief. But she found her albino friend sound asleep. Sinking back onto her calves, Elunai let out her own sigh and lowered her head to her palms. "How is this possible..."

"This isn't the first time?" Jikyshu asked.

She shook her head. "I don't really understand it, though. The last few...I didn't see any signs of injuries. They just...suffered...and then died. Yet there was an actual mark of attack on Fehln. Why was it different?"

"The curse can manifest in different ways. We usually see the physical effects under particularly aggressive circumstances. I'm not surprised this happened on a night like this."

Elunai fisted her hands in her hair again.

"So, you can communicate with animals?" came the next question.

She nodded. "Don't know why. Just can."

The man shrugged. "Some are born with it. I know a few like that back home."

Elunai's head shot up. "You do? Where are you from?" What a place that must be. She began to wonder if this traveler might have answers to her most burning questions.

There was that smile again. "A secluded land far from here...with daystar tonics and wildlife whisperers."

And there was that vague answer again.

Elunai felt her lips purse unintentionally. Turning from him, she began to gently collect Fehln into her hem. "You can stay. Feel free to use the garden and fire. There's extra wood in the stable." With that, she stood and turned for the cottage, handing him the rounded cup on her way. "Here...thank you for your help."

Jikyshu held up his hand to refuse the cup. "Please, keep it. That was brought for you anyway."

Elunai slowly retracted her hand and looked down at the piece. For the first time, she noticed the polished ceramic was intricately adorned with branched blossoms, much like the ones from her apple tree. "Are you sure? This looks... *extremely* valuable."

The man nodded, his kindly eyes glinting in the fire's glow. "Life is extremely valuable. And you're greatly assisting mine."

Elunai nodded to him and headed for the front door. Her mind couldn't shake how much more value he had already provided than she, wondering just how and why it had all come about in the manner it did.

CHAPTER 7

The morning was warm.

Copper and blonde poured over Elunai's face as she stared down at the open journal in her bedsheet-covered lap. The pages had teardrop-sized wrinkles in a few spots that had already dried, and a quill hung loosely from her right hand.

She had gotten sleep, but not much.

Fehln was still deep in slumber next to her pillow, the morning light glistening against his ivory fur from the bedroom windows. Aside from petting, sleeping on human beds was another thing he preferred not to engage in; however, that was the best way she could keep an eye on him through the night. No matter how much they bickered, jabbed, and pretended to moderately tolerate each other, she could not fathom her life in the glade without his grounding presence.

Elunai could see the woods beyond the warm curtain of daystar rays through her window and stared out at them almost lifelessly. She'd about given up trying to make sense of all that curse had put her through.

A light creak sounded from the kitchen. As she turned to see what it was, Pikan bounded in through her bedroom door.

"Elunai...!" he squeaked, "That new traveler asked me to come get you. Says he needs your help with somethin' important."

"How did you get in here...?"

"Uh...through the kitchen window..."

The maiden's thoughts spun wildly as she clearly remembered the window opened outward, not inward, and the physics it would take for such a small creature to pry it loose were... She shook her head. "Mm...so...he can talk to you, too?" she asked, moving on to the next conundrum.

"Well, he can speak to us, but I don't really think he understands us."

"Hm..."

"So...are ya comin'? How's Fehln?"

"Annoyed," came the other rodent's groggy voice.

Elunai and Pikan looked over to witness the albino finally stirring. He really was going to be fine after all.

"Why all the talking...why am on this bed...why did you pet me last night...?" Fehln asked, only half opening his eyes.

Elunai's lips pulled into a side pucker as she turned and hid a growing smile. "So, this important thing...did he say what it was?," she asked. Closing her journal, she set it and the quill upon the nightstand and swung her legs over the side of the bed.

"Somethin' about cargo he needed stored...I think?" Pikan replied.

Strange. No one had ever asked her for storage before, aside from shelter for horses. "Okay...I'll be out in a bit. Oh, and tell the others I'll be out with feed soon," she said, reaching for her wrap cape on the footboard.

Pikan took his leave and made sure to close the kitchen window behind him.

"Am I dead? Are you two just ignoring me?" Fehln's voice slurred.

Elunai slowly leaned back and glanced at him over her shoulder as she pulled her hair into a loose, side ponytail. "Go back to sleep, troublemaker."

"Or what..."

Elunai placed a knee on the edge of the mattress and leaned across the bed with an outstretched hand in full pet mode.

"*No...*" he snapped.

Her hand stopped just above his head. He was still too weak to move much, and she decided against subjecting him to a fate he couldn't resist...again; although, the taunt was well worth the reaction.

"I'll bring you food and water as soon as I can," she said as she retreated. "Seriously, though...rest."

She all but ignored the flurry of reprimands hurled in her direction as she made her way across the ridged flooring and out into the open air.

"Ah, good morning!" Jikyshu hailed. He was sitting at the garden rock table like he lived there.

Elunai took a moment to process the scene. His tent was modest enough and fit perfectly on the patio between the fire pit and the crop garden. Apparently, he had arrived with some kind of nuts or seeds as the breakfast crew was already enjoying themselves next to him. He'd even brought his own wooden stool, atop which he was sitting and peeling an orange.

An *orange*.

Elunai's gaze glued to the bright fruit in his hands for an unintentionally long moment. Truly, she could not remember the last time she'd seen one. "Are those... also from your homeland...?" she asked.

"Oh, this? Maybe..." he responded, picking up on her tone. "Want one?"

He didn't need to ask twice. Elunai made her way down the steps and across the stone walkway as quickly as her tired feet would carry her. An outstretched hand bearing said, plump citrus was waiting for her at the other end of the patio, and she quickly snatched it up. That peel didn't stand a chance - large pieces of it were chucked into the brushes in short order as Jikyshu looked on in amusement.

"You can eat the rind, you know," he said.

"That's not what I'm here for." A stream of orange juice crept down the corner of her mouth.

Apples satisfied a certain kind of fruity craving when the tree made them available. But oranges... If a daystar ray had a flavor, oranges certainly captured every bit of its sweet divinity.

Before she had finished enjoying her best breakfast in years, Jikyshu produced a wooden box from his pack and held it up for Elunai to see. "The chipmunk may have told you? We'll just need this stashed away somewhere cool before the day gets too warm," he explained.

She'd definitely forgotten about the 'important thing' he needed help storing. Stuffing the last bit of orange passed her lips, Elunai licked her fingers free of the remnants and then wiped her hands across the bottom of her tunic.

The man before her let another smile cross his features as she reached out to take the box from him.

The container wasn't much bigger than a few stacked books, but she needed both hands to bear its weight. And then, shock. "It's so cold...!" she exclaimed.

Jikyshu nodded. "There's ice in it."

Elunai's eyes widened. Lifting the lid, she found the inside of the box was lined in metal and stuffed to the brim with large chunks of solid ice. She glanced back up and found him beaming at her. Something about his countenance made her pause. He didn't simply smile a lot, she noticed...there was actually a level of care hidden behind those eyes she hadn't registered before. But how could that be? She was sure they'd never met.

"Think we can save it?" he asked.

The girl's face warmed as she averted her gaze. Quickly nodding, she turned on heel and ran back for the cottage.

"Hey, feel free to use it! Probably a good day for it..." he called after her.

Bursting through the front door, Elunai headed for the food cellar hatch across the kitchen. Kneeling next to it, she let herself breathe for just a moment. Wisps of hair settled about her flushed cheeks for a count of three inhales before she pulled the hatch open. Once the ice box was securely nestled in the cooling confines of the underground compartment, the maiden glanced over at the pitchers on the counter. Her mind finally processed what the traveler had given her permission to do.

"*Iced* felici-tea..." she said excitedly.

Quiet, safe, company-graced warmth. Those were the days she lived for.

Elunai turned a sprig of freshly-picked mint about in her fingers before dropping it into the iced beverage beside her. Fehln sat quietly atop her leg as she held up a piece of the frozen goodness for him to enjoy as it melted.

Two glass pitchers of tea, one red and one green, steeped in full exposure to the daystar atop one of the pickling barrels by the chimney. The voices of the maiden and traveler could be heard conversing softly over small, lap tasks and tea cups at the garden rock. Despite her desire to protect such a work of art, in a gesture of gratitude, Elunai opted to use the ornate cup Jikyshu had brought for her. He, on the other hand, requested glassware.

Fehln's ice eventually dissipated, and Elunai wiped her hand on her sundress before reaching back over for her own chilled beverage. Broken lumps of ice gently brushed against her top lip, renewing a much-missed rush of glee as she drank. Felici-tea, *indeed*.

A thick set of needle and thread passed back and forth between Jikyshu's fingers as he fortified a thinning patch on his travel bag. "It's hard to believe how warm it gets here. Do you get rain in the summer?" he asked.

"Sometimes. But it only ever rains at night. Same with the snow in winter."

"Huh...!" the man exclaimed. "Now that's interesting."

"Sometimes I wish it would rain in the daytime so I wouldn't have to water the crops as much, but...we really do need the daystar's light. The forest seems calmer with it shining."

"So, when did you come to live here in the haven?" His tone was casual, but Elunai's expression darkened.

Fehln looked up at her with a knowing gaze, wondering how she would answer that time.

The girl sighed. "I don't know," she said. "Honestly...my memory's hazy beyond about five years ago. I've just been here on my own...I think for a really long time."

Jikyshu's hands lowered a bit as they paused their work. "Huh..." he mused, much less enthusiastically. "You ever consider venturing out? Maybe moving somewhere with other people?"

A familiar churn stirred in Elunai's stomach. There she was, talking to someone she'd just met, and yet that question continued to manifest from traveler to traveler. Her gaze met Fehln's, and the honesty ended there. "I'm satisfied here, actually. This is where I've built a steady life with the only companions I can remember."

"I see." The man looked back down to his handiwork. "Truthfully, I think I'd go stir crazy after a while. As beautiful as this meadow is, I'd probably start to feel a bit trapped by it."

Trapped.

The word echoed as a shrill ring throughout Elunai's mind. She resonated with the sentiment beyond comfort. "If...I wanted to visit your homeland someday...unlikely, but hypothetically...which way would I travel?"

His smile widened. "South."

"And...once I go south, what landmarks should I look for?"

"A lot of trees."

"And once I'm beyond the trees?" Her brow twitched.

"A really, really big tree...and more trees."

Fehln stifled a cackle that nearly choked him.

Elunai took a deep swig of her chilled, green tea, not taking her eyes off the man before her. Her next inclination was to slam the cup back down, but promptly reconsidered. "Is your home in the woods?"

"Not particularly," he told her, a playful glint in his eye.

Elunai drew in a sharp breath. "Am I allowed to visit?"

"By all means, please! I'd love to have you, in fact-"

"Then why can't you tell me how to get there?!" she nearly cried.

Jikyshu's grin faded as he recomposed himself. "Because the way you get there will be entirely up to you."

"What does that mean?" she asked.

"It means...you must first decide to leave this place. And then, out there, you'll find your own way." He nodded toward the tree line.

Elunai sank back on her log seat. His words were just like Mister Keamotus's, only flavored a bit differently. That's when she knew every one of her questions would be ultimately futile. With a sharpness to her voice, she finally changed the subject, admitting to the man that it had been years since she'd last seen ice outside of the winter months.

"I was up north before I came here," Jikyshu told her, a bit wary of the change, "and those woods sure provide enough shade to keep it cold."

Elunai again pondered the possibility, or rather, the impossibility of the wooded world providing any kind of benefit. She found herself studying the man once more, trying to learn anything else about him through his features. His expression appeared soft and carefree despite his claimed life experience. His hands seemed relatively youthful as well, yet calloused - particularly at the upper palms of each hand. And there was something about listening to him talk that she decided was...pleasant? Too bad he was just as vague in his conversation as everyone else.

Gently scooping Fehln into her arms, the girl stood. "I need to tend the rest of my chores before it gets too late. There are made beds in the loft if you'd like to stay inside tonight. And and the well pump is out behind the stable by the stream."

Elunai didn't look at Jikyshu as she took her leave, but if she had, she would've seen the most defeated expression he'd allowed himself since arrival.

CHAPTER 8

Starset arrived just as Elunai was finishing up with the evening dishes. Fehln insisted on accompanying her to light the lanterns that night despite his ongoing recovery. From the looks of it, she was willing to go through with the task with much less abandon than previously, but he was still adamant that she needed a voice of reason with her.

"I never heard such a squeaky a voice of reason..." the girl mumbled as they made their way across the clearing.

"Well, take it in. This is your *hero* speaking!" he squeaked directly into her ear.

"You didn't save me, okay? You were being stupid." The words left a sting in her throat. She didn't mean that...not really. His ability to bring out the unabashed snark in her was masterful.

The two were soundless as the southern lamps were lit. Moving from one lantern to the next, Elunai wasn't sure if the air was growing thick with the forest's evil or the uncomfortable silence between her and the friend she had very nearly lost the night before.

Finally, on the trek east, she broke that silence...and her pride. "I'm sorry. I was being stupid..."

He registered the softness in her voice and glanced over to see the girl's eyes glistening wildly in the torchlight. Those same eyes focused intently on the next set of lanterns before them - determined to shut out the woods beyond. Fehln turned to keep watch over the foreboding thicket in her stead. Without her brashness, the darkness didn't seem nearly as roused that evening. He waited patiently, steadying himself squarely atop her left shoulder as she worked.

"You really didn't..." he spoke after the final lamp was warm with light.

"Didn't what...?" she asked, "Act stupid?"

"Oh, no, you were definitely far out of your right mind. But..."

Elunai pursed her lips and kept silent as she waited for him to finish.

"You didn't really want to die."

At that, any notion of a retort extinguished. Lowering the torch to the stream, Elunai doused the flame, and the two headed back toward the garden.

Perhaps she hadn't *truly* wanted the curse to claim her life. But what exactly was one to do without the faintest idea of how to continue on under the circumstances?

"What good am I, Fehln...?" she asked him quietly as they drew nearer to the fire pit. "I can't wield light...not for myself or others. And souls are dying for it."

The squirrel hesitated in his answer. Having attempted encouragement many times in the past, his words seemed to consistently fall on ears unwilling to listen and a heart set on its own perceptions. Even so, he had a hard time blaming the girl as both suffering and death had very real, very loud, and very frequent voices in their midst.

Elunai did need a voice of reason. But more than that...she needed a voice of hope - just as consistent, if not more-so than the unrelenting cries of despair.

"Your light touches more than you realize, Elunai. Just ask them." Fehln motioned toward the small cluster of animals at the fireside.

"The ones I *failed*...?" she inquired.

Even if he'd had time to respond before they joined the others, Fehln sealed his chops in a clear bout of frustration.

Elunai quietly sat herself down beside Pikan and the sparrows. Her eyes trailed over to the flower beds, taking in the newly-bloomed cosmos and marigold amongst the roses. Those bright colors really did provide the most convenient distraction.

"We figured you might be headed to bed after the lantern run," Pikan said, "You've had a busy day."

She shook her head. "I don't really like sleeping indoors when a stranger is staying..."

Jikyshu had opted to retire up in the loft that night. Though he had thus far proven his trustworthiness, Elunai still wanted to keep her distance.

Fehln carefully slid off of her shoulder and settled onto the fire-warmed patio at her side. "Wait a minute," he mused, "what about Zei? You didn't seem to have any problems sleeping inside when she first came around."

"Zeidys was different..."

At that, Lei's curiosity got the best of her. "How so?"

Glancing out at the brightening array of night stars overhead and grateful for the change of subject, Elunai eased into the tale of the paladin she had met from the west.

Nothing typically came from that end of the glade. Not even the forest's curse attempted to spill in from anywhere but the established roads. But that woman had appeared from the most unbeaten path imaginable, if one could even call it that. She'd certainly made it a path for herself.

The contrast of long, black hair against white armor is what had struck Elunai first before the tall steed appeared at the woman's side. Then, the air of gentle yet steadfast resolve that exuded from the warrior as she spoke set Elunai's senses at a peace the girl hadn't known before.

"She told me that she'd renewed the barrier surrounding the clearing. I hadn't even realized there was one," Elunai admitted. "Did you all know about it?"

Each creature, save for Fehln, shook their heads.

Her back lowered to the patio, gaze returning to the sky as she continued her story. "Apparently, there's some kind of hidden shield that keeps the curse from overtaking the haven when the daystar is away, except where the roads are. That's why the lanterns are there."

Elunai went on to describe Zeidys's mysterious mission as part of some division of warriors specially trained and charged with containing malevolent threats across the land. She could even heal souls who'd been harmed by the forest's curse with her own light and was the one who'd given Elunai the guidebook on that ability.

The girl had found an unexpected companionship after the woman's offers to help around the cottage, keep Elunai company for days on end, and even light the lanterns at starset. Then, there was the pressure.

"She just kept *pushing...*" the girl said, her hand curling into a light fist behind her head. "More-so than anyone else I'd met, and I couldn't figure out why - she seemed so nice."

"Pushing...what?" Phel asked.

"Me. To leave this place. Convinced it's my 'prison'. She said it again the last time I saw her, and that was when she gave me the Stelluvak Star. It was still shining then... That was two years ago."

"Keep it lit..." came Fehln's hushed voice. "That's what the lady told Elunai before she left."

"The brooch? But how...?" asked Pikan.

"She was adamant that I was suppressing a radiance of my own..." Elunai sullenly replied. "Clearly, she was wrong."

Fehln glanced back up at the maiden from the corner of his eye, his expression one of weary disappointment. He drew in a long breath. "Well," he sighed, "kinda hard to tell if you never wear it." The accusation in his tone wasn't held back in the slightest.

Elunai sat up. "It shouldn't matter if I wear it or not," she said. "Zei could keep it alight just by being near it. I've never come close to being able to do that...or anything else she did for that matter."

The albino issued his signature eye roll, officially giving up on the matter for the evening. "I'm turning in," he announced, stretching out his legs. He winced only slightly at the pang still healing on his backside.

"You can take the bed tonight - I won't be in there," Elunai said, ignoring his dismissal.

"Nope. My evergreen's calling."

She watched him saunter off toward his hideaway in the trunk of a nearby pine.

"Elunai..." Pikan spoke up, "Hope y'know I don't hold it against you...my mate's death."

The girl's eyes widened only slightly, but the sparrows caught the effect.

Phel made a small hop toward her. "True," he said, "our friend's passing wasn't your fault either. Lei and I should be off to the branches as well, but you need know, friend...we're grateful for your kindness."

"Always...that's why we like spending time here," Lei agreed.

Without waiting for a response, the two birds nodded to Elunai and Pikan and quietly fluttered off to find their evening perch.

"Will you be a'ight out here on your own...?" Pikan asked.

Elunai had fixed her bewildered stare on the paving stones, still processing the confessions. There were no indications she even heard the little one speaking.

"Okay...well...y'know where to find me if you...happen to need anythin' from a chipmunk." Pikan slowly rose to his feet and watched the girl a moment longer before heading out to the old stump in the field.

～ .∴ ✧ ∴. ～

The night was a bit chilled for a summer evening. Even with the fire pit alight, Elunai felt the need to procure a blanket from indoors.

There were no signs of Jikyshu awakening as she pulled a thick cover from her bed and wrapped it around her shoulders. She had half the mind to simply slip between the sheets over the mattress and claim a much needed and much more comfortable rest that night, but the thought of sleeping in closer proximity to the unfamiliar traveler caused her to head back outside.

Besides...a night outside would guarantee she slept lightly in case of an unexpected threat - from him or otherwise.

Quietly closing the front door behind her, Elunai headed down the rickety steps over the porch. Reaching the pavement, she froze.

55

Far too near to Pikan's tree stump, the girl beheld a flicker of orange fur, only illuminated by the outer reaches of the garden's firelight. She strained to see what exactly she was looking at, not completely convinced her mind wasn't betraying her.

Then, the flash of a reflective eye confirmed she was indeed staring at a living creature sitting there. Slowly, her sight adjusted.

That wasn't just any creature. That was a *cat*. A *real* one of domesticated size. One she'd never seen before. Worried that it might be looking for Pikan, she addressed it firmly, "What're you doing there...?"

No response.

Moving closer, Elunai spoke again, "Don't you disturb the little ones around here...leave them alone." That's when she realized...the feline had only one eye, and a dark, half closed socket sat where the other had once been. She pulled back a step, mortified, and her mind started down the spiral of how that may have come about.

Finally, the cat spoke quietly, "I heard...that I could find some food here." He sounded hesitant and exhausted.

"You..." Elunai started. Her thoughts turned to where and from whom he could've heard such a thing.

The panther...maybe?

She stood there a moment longer, locked in a stare-down with the one-eyed cat, as she considered his weary state. In calming her initial fear, the maiden beheld a truly bereft animal, tired, and clearly untrusting of his surroundings.

Clutching the blanket tighter around her shoulders, Elunai turned back to the cottage. "Wait there, please...I'll be right back."

To her surprise, the cat obeyed. He didn't move an inch from where he was sitting as she disappeared into her home and reemerged minutes later with a plate of dried trout.

"I was saving this for lunch tomorrow...but you're welcome to it." Elunai set the plate down at the edge of the stone patio.

The orange feline backed away slightly as she came near despite the enticing scent of fish.

Weak and timid though the cat seemed, the girl still didn't trust him near Pikan's new home. "No...here," she said. She retreated to the bottom of the steps. "I'll sit back here so you can eat."

A flash of light caught the cat's attention from indoors, though it faded just as quickly as it came. He stared intently at the large common room window long enough for Elunai to look back in wonder.

"What is it...?" she asked. When she returned a forward gaze, her guest had visibly relaxed and was ravenously lapping up the plated trout she'd shared.

Despite her confusion, Elunai's heart began to ache for the soul in front of her, her mind slipping back to a flurry of thoughts of what might have befallen him. He was desperately famished. Perhaps he was completely lost out there in the woods. Slowly, her chin lowered to her knees as she watched and whispered, "Everything's going to be okay..."

He looked up at her only once as he ate his meal to completion, hardly coming up for breath. When the fish was gone, the cat sat back and licked about his chops, seemingly searching for anything else he could eat.

"I'm sorry...that's all I have tonight," the maiden apologized. "But you're welcome to rest here. It's safe. And I can catch some more fish tomorrow."

The cat shook his head and backed away once again. "I ought to be going..."

A pang shot through Elunai's chest. "Really, you can stay. The others will be cautious, but...we'll figure it out. I can make a patch for your eye. We'll get you well." The sudden, powerful need to protect him from whatever else might await in the forest began to overwhelm her. "I could use some company by the fire this evening, actually...my friends have all gone to sleep."

There was a pause as the feline reluctantly considered her plea and wondered if it was more for his benefit or hers. His gaze wandered back over to the window one more time. "Alright," he said, "for the night."

Pushing unshed tears from the corners of her eyes, Elunai nodded, relieved... and hopeful.

CHAPTER 9

The incessant nudging of tiny paws, no...*claws* stirred Elunai from sleep just as the daystar was reemerging over the treetops.

She squinted her eyes open just slightly enough to register the bright outline of leaves and a squirrelly silhouette. A moan sounded in her throat, her body aching from a short night's rest on the pavement. Thank goodness for that plush blanket wrapped all the way around her.

"You should get up. That traveler's getting ready to leave," came Fehln's voice.

Realities of the waking world hit all at once, and she bolted upright. "Cat..." she voiced, hoarsely. But a quick glance across the garden rendered her evening guest nowhere to be found. Her heart sank.

"Cat?" Fehln asked, suddenly on high alert.

The maiden did her best to hide the welling distress and shook her head. "Maybe...a dream." She brought a hand up to comb slender fingers through her tousled, fire pit-smelling hair as Jikyshu appeared from the cottage.

"Good morning!" he beamed, "Wish I'd known you were camping out last night, I'd have offered my tent." He smiled so warmly she nearly forgot what she was worried about. He adjusted the large pack on his shoulders and Elunai realized he was completely ready to go. It seemed so sudden.

"W-would you like any breakfast? I can get something together here shortly..." she asked.

"Oh, no, I'm alright - but thank ya! Need an early start to get where I'm going," he replied.

Visibly perturbed, Elunai pushed herself to her feet and did her best to dust off the wrinkled tunic hanging from her tired form. She was not looking forward to yet another goodbye to soon. Her gait felt a bit off kilter as she followed just behind the man across the clearing to the southern border where the lamps were still fizzling out from the night before. She studied him from the side, for the first time noting how his hair fell lightly about the defined contours of his face and the broad shoulders that held up that travel pack. "So...uh...are you headed home?" she asked.

He smiled again, turning to her just before the edge of the forest. "Something like that." The pure disdain on her face drew a nervous chuckle from him. "What?" he asked.

Her rebuke never sounded. Somehow, his kind expression calmed her thoughts as quickly as they'd heated. "Nothing...I'd just really like to get my hands on more of that tonic you shared..."

There was a smirk from him then - the likes of which she hadn't seen up to that point. "You're welcome to join me," he said.

The girl startled. The gleam in his eyes, those words...utterly unexpected, and yet something rendered them powerfully enticing. For a moment, and only a moment, her aversion to the woods escaped her. But then, "I...I'm not ready," she told him. She surprised even herself by not giving him a flat out 'no,' but reality settled again as her mind flew through the logistics of the endeavor...and the forest reentered her thoughts.

She saw it then, the subtle look of defeat in his gaze. Not disappointment as much as it was a genuine sadness that he didn't let linger.

"Miss Elunai...thank you kindly for the shelter of your haven and sweet hospitality. Should we meet again, I'd love to sit and talk with you more." Jikyshu lowered in a slight bow. He flashed a final, encouraging smile her way before turning down the wooded road.

"Who told you my name?" she asked in a hurry.

He waved a hand up in the air and without facing her called, "Your friends! Lovely bunch!"

"What?!"

He didn't respond as the darkness thickly shrouded his form into nothing.

Elunai slammed her foot against the weathering cobblestone beneath her. He had her ability! And couldn't even bother to mentioned it or stay and... "Augh!" A heavy breath escaped her lungs as she turned to head back to the cottage, but just before her gaze left the woods, something bright caught her eye.

At first, she thought she'd imagined it, but then a shimmer reappeared between a pair of thick, upraised tree roots just beyond the clearing.

Her curiosity piqued.

Crouching, the girl's hand moved ever so slightly toward the roots, hesitating. She could feel it. Whatever foul essence lurked in the shadows of the wooded world loomed near...always watching.

Fear rose up to match her curiosity in intensity. Even so, she could see the tip of the shiny object protruding just out of reach from where she was and she fixed her gaze on it like a lifeline. She *had* to uncover it.

In a burst of daring, Elunai lunged forward, grabbed the shining thing, and then pushed herself back into the clearing with as much strength as her adrenalin-ridden legs could manage. Luckily, the object went with her.

A moment of stillness passed, filled only with the sound of the girl's breathing.

Once certain that she wasn't dead or dying, Elunai let her line of sight move to the thing in her hand. Just as she did, the brilliant, golden feather dissipated into thin air.

Weeks passed in a haze of heat and as much indoor-time as possible.

Elunai had far too much time to think to herself. She never saw the orange cat again, and her thoughts became consumed by the strange feather she'd found at the edge of the woods, which she assumed belonged to the goldfinch, but never brought it up with her companions.

What she *had* brought up, however, was how they'd never told her they could communicate with Jikyshu as clearly as they could with her. Pikan ended up a stammering mess trying to explain how the traveler had sworn them to secrecy.

Everything surrounding those recent events was deeply strange and frustrating.

In an attempt to distract herself from things she couldn't understand or control, the green-eyed maiden defied one sweltering afternoon and busied herself one day in the construction of a simple, plank swing.

She'd found some extra rope and a good-looking piece of flat firewood in the stable from her last haul. The brace and bit drill she'd reluctantly traded a bushel of apples for finally came in handy, and the swing was pieced together in relatively short order.

Fehln's old, red pine sat just beyond the garden patio beside the cottage and was one of the only trees situated within the safer confines of the glade. Its thick, lower branches were high enough up off the ground to hang a swing from, but getting up there was going to be the challenge.

Elunai looked around the field for the means to climb the trunk with the swing in hand without injuring herself. Her gaze landed on a couple of doves enjoying a midday meal in the millet patch. They never really spoke to her much - seemingly content with eating the food she provided and keeping their distance. Regardless, the thought still crossed her mind to ask them to assist with the rope.

Just as she opened her mouth, the unmistakable sound of high-pitched arguing reached her ears, growing louder and louder as a couple of rodents returned from their forest run.

Elunai glanced over to witness Fehln and Miiskoe dragging a fresh haul of mushrooms out from the bushes. "Oh..! They're growing already?" she asked, setting the swing down and sauntering over to lift their burden. The sight of the delectable fungi made her realize the corn was almost ready for harvest as well.

"Alright, where is it?" Miiskoe snapped at the albino.

"I dunno." Fehln shrugged.

The grey one seethed a bit more fiercely than usual. "Produce the nut..."

"Or what..."

The world's squeakiest battle cry was cut short as Elunai grabbed Miiskoe by the scruff of his neck and brought him up to look her in the eyes. "What's this about, Sir...?" she asked, suppressing a smirk.

He wriggled in her grasp a moment before conceding to her stronger grip. "He *said* he'd found a walnut! Swore to the daystar and back I could have it if I helped him get your snacks - that slimy, lying piece of-"

"Really?" Elunai rolled her eyes over at Fehln. "A walnut?"

Fehln shrugged again. "I found those mushrooms you liked and needed the labor. Not my fault he's dumb enough to believe that story."

Miiskoe began writhing again and cursing up a storm.

Elunai sighed. They all knew walnuts only came with Zeidys when she visited. The fact that Miiskoe had fallen for the ruse was, indeed, a tragedy. Even so...the mushrooms were probably worth it.

"Let me go, woman! I'll *wreck* that pasty quack!"

"Miiskoe..." Elunai said, "Thank you for helping with the snacks. I will deal with Fehln. When I let you go-"

"He's dead!"

The girl's expression fell into one of quiet annoyance. She pointed at Fehln. "You stay right there." Then, as quickly as possible without dropping the squirming animal, Elunai made her way indoors.

Miiskoe's fervent antics continued until he laid eyes on the spread Elunai had prepared on the kitchen table. "What's this...?" he asked as she plopped him down in front of it.

"The other snacks. Help yourself," she said.

Carrots, cucumbers, spinach, roasted trout, and the array of tree nuts gathered by the squirrels earlier that month covered nearly half of the large dining table.

Elunai emptied the sack of mushrooms into a bowl on the counter and filled it halfway with water to wash them as Miiskoe picked up a sliced carrot.

"You sure about this?" he asked. He was hesitant to dig in knowing how much work she put into her harvest and preparation.

"I'm fine," she said, "there's about to be a whole lot more where that came from. Have you seen the apple tree?" With a growing smile on her lips, the maiden placed a wooden dish of cleaned morels in front of the quieted rodent. "Eat up."

That time, Miiskoe obliged, decidedly content at the compromise for Fehln's blunder.

Leaving that squirrel to his meal, Elunai headed back out to confront the other. "Hey!" she called, catching the albino filing his teeth on the plank swing.

He looked up at her, mouth still on the bark.

"Seriously? Does that *look* like it's for biting?"

Fehln sat up, cleaning his chops. "Sure does."

Elunai knelt and grabbed one of the rope ends, holding it up to him. "I think you've caused enough trouble for one day."

"Yeah, well you're welcome for my entire idea to get you those mushrooms. What's this?"

"My entire idea to get this swing hung up. Take this part up to that branch. I'll tell you how to secure it once you're there." Elunai pointed to the thick base of the pine's lowest overhang.

"You really think I'm your lackey..."

"No. I think you pick too many fights and could use just as much of a distraction as I can."

Fehln returned her glare with equal ferocity until the weariness in her gaze became apparent. He looked up at the tree and then back at the rope end. There were clearly two pieces of rope that would have to go up, and the job wouldn't be quick considering what he was. However, he did seem like the most viable solution.

"And you trust me with this?" he asked.

"With my whole swinging future."

CHAPTER 10

The daystar's shining hours began to wane, and the stars of night became more constant companions as Elunai fully committed to harvest and preparing for winter. The rains began to fall at night, and she'd concurrently begun keeping the front room fireplace lit through the evening.

Baskets of apples, peas, and dried sunflowers covered the kitchen floor. A parchment list lay atop the table with hay, potatoes, garlic, and onions still waiting to be crossed off under the completed 'corn' item.

Hot green tea sat next to the list in the ceramic cup Jikyshu had gifted, waiting for its owner to return from working outdoors in the cooling air.

The final bundle of hay was dropped onto low, wooden shelving inside the small field stable to the east of the cottage. Elunai brushed remnants of the grass off her sleeves before hanging the sickle up on its hook. A quiet moment passed as she took the opportunity to breathe, sweat careening down the sides of her face in streams despite the evening chill. Then, she closed the gate behind her as she stepped out, rolling up her sleeves, wiping her brow, and picking up a basket of freshly-gathered corn to add to the kitchen collection.

Twilight had nearly ended, but the colors she could still see in the surrounding trees by the lamplight caused her to pause. The colors...were all blurred together. Elunai blinked a few times in an attempt to clear her vision, but it didn't seem to help. Maybe the lamps were dimmer than usual? She made a mental note to ask the next traveler for more oil whenever possible.

The maiden slowly made her way back to the cottage. Perhaps it was the early fading of the daystar, but she felt unnaturally tired for that point in the evening. As she reached the edge of the patio, her foot suddenly caught on one of the stones.

Corn flew up everywhere as the girl went down.

Fehln and Pikan looked up from their conversation by the stump as Elunai hit the pavement. They scurried to her side as quickly as their petite legs would carry them.

"What happened? Elunai!" Fehln asked.

She couldn't figure it out. Her head was swimming, but she was sure she hadn't hit it. Vision blurring further, Elunai tried to raise herself up, but her arms refused to bear her weight.

Her companions were frantic, looking her up and down for signs of injury.

"I can't tell if she's hurt..." Pikan said, sniffing around. In the chilling weather, the maiden had begun wearing hose pants under her long-sleeved tunics, making it nearly impossible to detect minor wounds. "Can't smell any blood, at least."

Elunai managed to crawl her way to the first step in front of the cottage and prop herself up, but still couldn't stand.

"Elunai...what's wrong?" Fehln repeated. "Are you hurt? Do you need water?"

As the girl tried to answer affirmatively, she felt what energy she had left drain from her body. Slumping onto the step, she heard her friends calling out to her just before fading from consciousness.

A rush of hot and cold surged through her body.

The sensation slowly drew Elunai's eyes open just enough to catch the blurred, flickering reflection of an oil lamp's light on the ceiling of her bedroom.

Her heartbeat quickened as she regained consciousness and ransacked her memory to make sense of the situation. Then, she felt the ache. Her entire body felt as though she'd been crushed by a boulder, and her jaw slackened as the feel of a dry, scratchy throat came into play.

Elunai was covered to the neck in heavy sheets, and there was a wet cloth resting over her forehead.

She finally gathered the strength to move after a moment and turned her head toward the doorway. There was a stool and a bucket of water by her bed.

Something cold poked an exposed part of her forehead and she startled - a sharp intake of breath sounding through her nose.

"Still feverish..." she heard Fehln's voice say.

Then, the sound of human footsteps filtered through the doorway.

Elunai suddenly found herself staring up into a pair of piercing, hazel eyes illuminated by the flame on her nightstand.

The woman with long, raven-black hair gestured toward Fehln. "I was on my way here when this one came out into the forest." That voice was low and calm, and Elunai felt a long-forgotten ease instantly wash over her at the sound of it. "I don't understand them as you do, but I got the idea."

"Zei..." Elunai breathed as the older woman lowered herself to the stool. It was then that the girl noticed the armor and sword leaning up against the wall by the bedroom entryway.

There was a soft smile in Zeidys's eyes. "Stryk appreciates the fresh hay," she said.

Elunai finally remembered what she'd been doing right before her fall and found it ironic that the paladin and her horse showed up right after the stable was ready. "It's like you knew..." she said quietly.

Zeidys let a smirk pull at her lips and told Elunai she knew what time of year it was.

Elunai took in a deep breath and went to rise, but was promptly stopped by both the squirrel and the woman.

"I already brought in your corn. I'll get your tea. You're staying right there for the night," Zeidys declared.

Elunai had forgotten how firm the warrior could be and felt confused on how to respond. She watched as the older woman left the room. Then, the girl let her head fall back onto the pillow, unexpected tears collecting at the corners of her eyes.

"You in pain?" Fehln asked.

Elunai shook her head. While her body did still ache, it was her spirit in deepest distress. "I...thought I was doing it right... I thought maybe...there was

a chance I could be as strong as her if I just kept fighting through each day.”

Zeidys returned with the tea and helped Elunai sit up to drink it. The paladin was silent, not betraying a single emotion in her expression as the girl continued with her confession.

“I read your book so many times, but can’t even save one life...” Elunai choked back a gulp of warm liquid. “I’m so, so tired of being like this.”

Sitting back on the stool, Zeidys asked, “Is that why you never wore the brooch?”

“I couldn’t...” Elunai glanced over at the eight-pointed star symbol on Zeidys’s breastplate, winced, and lowered her gaze to her tea cup.

“No...I suppose not with that frame of mind. I’ll take it back with me when-” Zeidys stopped as Elunai looked up in a panic. She met the girl’s green eyes with another subtle smirk. “Ah...okay.”

Fehln jumped off the headboard to the floor. “I’ll go update Pikan so he can sleep, then turn in myself. Glad we got you taken care of, kid...” he said.

The young woman nodded to him before he headed out through the kitchen window. “Thank you...” she whispered.

Zeidys picked up the cloth that had fallen from Elunai’s forehead and rung it out over the bucket, placing it on the rim, then rose to her feet. “We’ll talk more in the morning. In the meantime, get some rest...and maybe think about that whole lesson I taught you years ago,” she said. “Dream of it.”

Elunai didn’t respond, largely out of exhaustion, but her mind was turning that memory over and over.

The lamp was extinguished, and Zeidys headed back out into the front room.

CHAPTER II

The smell of citrus and rosemary brought Elunai back to her senses the next morning - the daystar already high in the sky.

She took a long while to rise, still feeling weak and in full swing of whatever illness had befallen her, but the smell of food she didn't have to prepare gave her enough energy to slowly swing her legs off the side of the mattress.

The girl was an absolute wreck. Messy hair, wrinkled clothing that still smelled of hay, and the most awful taste in her mouth. While noting how she needed to clean up, her gaze wandered over to the equipment still leaning against her bedroom wall.

In an unrestrained bout of curiosity, Elunai slowly made her way over to the sword and let her fingers graze the hilt. A sudden, jarring sense of weight befell her spirit, and she withdrew her hand with a gasp. The sensation felt as though every experience that blade had ever endured sent a resonating shock through her being. Zeidys never spoke much of her battles, but she had explained the gist of her charge to seek, subdue, and defend against what was evil in that world. For a moment, Elunai wondered why the wooded world was still so dark with people like Zei patrolling it.

Regaining her resolve, Elunai took the sword by its scabbard and pulled on the grip until the base of the dual-edged blade was free. For a weapon that had seen such unspeakable horrors, the metal was polished so brilliantly she could see herself in it, and it bore runes she didn't understand yet found strikingly beautiful.

That's when she heard Zeidys's voice outdoors.

Pushing the blade back into its casing, Elunai replaced the sword against the wall and headed out to the front room.

Through the large window by the fireplace, she watched Zeidys and Stryk out in the clearing running exercises. The woman was holding Elunai's staff like a horizontal obstacle as the horse practiced jumps over it.

For a moment, Elunai marveled at how the paladin made herself at home there - almost as though a long, lost sister had finally returned. Shifting her gaze to the kitchen counter, the girl caught sight of a warm cup of water, presumably waiting for her, imbued with the treasures fresh honey and lemon.

"I wonder where she found those..."

Sitting next to the cup were the final slices from her loaf that had been lightly toasted and spread with hummus, no doubt from the newly harvested chickpeas.

Making her way over to the enticing breakfast, Elunai noticed her baskets of fruits and vegetables were in the midst of being unloaded into the cellar. Her eyes then rested on an intricate lantern set on the table. She paused a moment to touch its delicate details. "I've never seen designs like this," she mused.

Her examination of the metal was suddenly interrupted by Zeidys coming through the front door.

"Eat up," the elder said.

Elunai tensed a bit, still unused to being commanded in her own home. Still, she got situated at the table, stomach groaning in agreement. A wave of bliss rolled over her at the first bite of toast. Even though her sense of taste was dulled under the influence of her illness, she could swear she tasted the faint saltiness of butter on that bread.

"Where's that lantern from?" she asked.

"Far away," was the clipped reply. Zeidys replaced the wooden staff against the inner corner of the door frame.

Elunai's cheeks puffed. "*Where*...is 'far away'...?" she prodded.

"Not here."

The younger woman drew in a deep breath through her nose and swallowed a sound gulp of lemon water.

"How're you feeling?" Zeidys asked.

"Like Stryk's feces."

"Hm... There's some of that in the field, by the way - careful where you step."

Elunai hid a slight eye roll behind her raised beverage. As relieved as she was to have that pair back at the haven, they'd certainly made sure to bring their... double edge.

Zeidys had settled on the bench across from Elunai at the table, and the girl could feel the elder's stare on her without even looking.

"What?" Elunai asked between bites.

"Do you really plan to stay here forever?"

Elunai's gut tightened. She'd prayed, desperately, for that question to never resurface. A fool's prayer. Her eyes briefly found the star brooch on the mantle - its edges lightly sparked with an elevated energy in the room. "Where would I go?" she asked, "I have no idea what's out there."

"And you won't until you embark." Zeidys's tone became increasingly impatient, and Elunai's rose to match.

"Why not? Why can't you just *tell* me?"

"It's not my journey."

"I don't...!" Elunai clipped her sentence to get a better handle on her frustration. "I don't understand," she sighed

"If you never leave here, you never will understand. Nor will you ever be anything more than you are now." At that, Zeidys rose from the table.

Elunai looked up to the paladin, horror streaking across her face. "Are you leaving?"

Hazel eyes full of firm benevolence looked back on Elunai. "This time, I'm not leaving until you decide who you want to be."

"Why do you care?"

"Because I do," the woman asserted. Zeidys grabbed the vegetable list and a few of the emptied baskets from a corner of the room and headed back out the door.

Elunai felt sick all over again as the door shut. She looked up as Fehln and Pikan entered through the open kitchen window above the counter. They held what appeared to

be chunks of carnival squash and walnuts in their mouths as they plopped down onto the bench next to her. So...Zei hadn't forgotten.

"How're you feeling?" Fehln asked after spreading his stash out in front of him.

She didn't answer. One last swig of lemon water later, Elunai got up from the table to head back to bed.

～ .⁺ ✧ ⁺. ～

Zeidys preferred to light the eastern lanterns first and finish up at the southern end of the clearing. She always made such quick work of them, one could assume she knew nothing of the threatening abyss beyond. That night, however, once her work was done, she paused to stare into the void of the wooded world. Her eyes flashed, expression severe, and stance firm as though challenging some unseen entity.

A cold wind began rustling the dying leaves and swept passed her face, pushing ebony locks ever so slightly out of place. She didn't move even as a subtle, dark mist formulated on the air current.

To anyone not listening for it, the hiss that suddenly addressed her would have sounded no different than the swaying of the tree branches.

"*The weak...must succumb...*" it rendered. "*Do not interfere...*"

"Still spewing that poison..." Zeidys murmured.

The apparition rushed the lantern on Zeidys's right and swiftly snuffed it out with an extended gust of wind.

Hand aglow, a forceful wave of the warrior's arm drove the intruding tendril back into the forest.

"The audacity," she growled. She proceeded to relight the lantern while watching the darkness retreat, fully realizing its intent amidst the haven. "A slow torment..."

Before turning back to the cottage, the woman caught the distinct, light-bearing train of the goldfinch's tail swiftly weaving through the darkened woods before her. Her eyes trained on the fading glow as her head lowered in a silent nod.

Zeidys followed the old, stone pathway back through the clearing. The torch was doused and set back in the stable as she bid a quick 'goodnight' to her steed.

Feminine, yet strong hands picked up a heavy pale of water at the foot of the steps as the woman reentered the small abode.

A large, wooden basin sat by the fireplace. Moving over to it, Zeidys emptied the contents of her bucket over the planked edge to finally fill the entire tub with fresh well water. Setting the pale aside, she headed into the back bedroom to fetch her sword.

"Hey...get yourself up. Bath is about ready," she told the barely-sleeping girl on the bed. The woman paused a moment before taking up her weapon, noticing it had been disturbed. She looked over at Elunai, an amused glint in her eye.

A groan, a stretch, and a messy head of copper and blonde stirred under the sheets as Elunai groggily turned toward the paladin. She watched through weary eyes as the woman left the room, drawing her blade. The girl thought she saw its frosted runes begin to glow a hot orange before Zeidys turned out of sight into the front room.

The shrill sound of sizzling hissed through the cottage and was soon replaced with gurgles of lightly bubbling water. Steam began to sift through the hallway as Zeidys reemerged, wiping her sword down with a cloth.

"I'm already dying...you don't have to boil me alive," Elunai mumbled.

Zeidys shot her an unamused look, replacing the sheathed weapon against the wall. "Leave your clothes by the front door. I'll take them out with the bedding," she said and began stripping the dirty sheets from the mattress.

The undressing process went as slowly as her other movements, and Elunai found her mind wandering. Why was Zei going so far to care for her that time? There seemed to be more to the gesture than the simple fact that the girl was sick, but nothing came up in conversation or appeared terribly different from previous visits.

Piling her clothes beside the door, as instructed, Elunai moved to pick up the bar of soap on the hearth before lightly dipping one toe into the basin.

Surprisingly, the water wasn't as hot as she'd expected. The energy that exuded from Zeidys's sword worked quickly and powerfully, but somehow hadn't overdone its task.

Elunai let herself slip all the way into the tub and marveled at the sensation. A full basin of perfectly heated water took her forever to draw - having to go back and forth from the well and heating each pot of water individually. She usually settled for rinsing off by the pump during the day. That bath, though...felt like the warmest embrace she'd ever experienced and only ever came about when Zei did.

Cupping water into her hands to wet her face and hair, Elunai heard the older woman moving about in the loft, noting that her manner seemed urgent - or perhaps simply laced with purposeful intent. Slowly, that viridescent gaze moved back to the hanging brooch as the girl continued washing.

Zeidys didn't descend the stairs until Elunai had finished with her bath and was drying off with the towel that had been placed beside the tub.

"Why are you doing all this?" Elunai asked as she squeezed her dripping hair between soft, cotton folds.

Zeidys sat down at the edge of the hearth, hairbrush in hand, and tapped the empty spot beside her for the girl to join.

Elunai pulled the towel tighter about her chest and obliged.

Running the brush carefully through those copper-blonde tresses, Zeidys responded, "I want you to be ready...and of the most sound mind possible. And there's something important I want to ensure you understand. Do you remember what I told you just before I left last time? When I gave you the star..."

"Mhm..." was Elunai's soft reply. Repeating that lesson was ever the difficulty.

At the girl's hesitation, the woman slowly voiced, "Light the night with relentless grit. Be the star that..."

"Keeps it lit..." Elunai finished.

Zeidys nodded despite how a subtle sadnesses weighed on her expression.

"I don't...have that ability, Zei..."

The brush hitched, catching on a tangle. Once it resolved, the woman shifted into Elunai's line of sight.

"You do," she said. "Y'know how I know that?"

The younger woman hesitantly shook her head, and warm hands rested gently on the sides of her shoulders.

"You have life. That gift is the mark of one who is divinely precious and purposeful. Nothing has the ability to change that about you."

The green in the girl's irises danced with orange and red light from the fireplace as she listened, contemplating.

"You have a choice. You can either accept who you're made to be as who you truly are, or reject it. Physical strength, intellect, prowess...none of those things matter in this decision. What you choose to believe about the foundations of your being will determine the *path* you take and the *destination*...you reach."

Elunai's eyes widened and a deep, slow breath pulled in through her lips.

"If you decide to accept, try reciting that lesson in first-person. Do it often and out loud, even if you don't believe it."

With that, Zeidys rose and made her way back to the kitchen end of the front room.

"Zei," Elunai called after her, "where does the curse come from?"

The elder woman paused a moment before beginning preparations for a meal. She didn't look back over at the girl, responding, "Some say it formed with the woods."

"And you? What do you think?"

"I think...the only thing you need to worry about is making that star shine."

CHAPTER 12

Dust sparkled on the daystar rays pouring through the kitchen window as Elunai rinsed a final dish over a water bucket. She felt a bit better after another night of rest in Zei's care. As her mentor had deemed the downstairs bed linens in need of washing, the girl had slept up in the loft on the second bed, which had granted an unexpected sense of security and peace. Her mind wandered to what things might be like if she more often kept the company of other human beings she knew and trusted.

Once again, her gaze shifted from the edge of the forest to the Stelluvak Star, where it lingered for a long moment.

What if...? What *then*...? What could really be...?

Pulling her hands from the pale and drying them on the hem of her tunic, Elunai made her way across the room. After a final moment of silent contemplation, she snatched the brooch up off its hook and fastened it to the upper left corner of her wrap cape.

Her hand rested over the smooth surface of the mysterious jewel as she inhaled deeply. Then, with a sound exhale, she headed outdoors as though nothing at all had changed.

The glade seemed quiet that day. Stryk was out grazing in the field while the other creatures kept themselves busy elsewhere. Zeidys was off doing...whatever it was she did when she wasn't around. Patrolling, perhaps.

Elunai made her way around the garden until she came to Fehln's tree. The albino didn't appear after a few moments, and she realized he must've been out with the others searching for more food. They'd need it...winter would settle in any day.

Grabbing one of the swing ropes, Elunai turned and seated herself lightly atop the plank. When she was confident it would still hold her weight, she let it bear her fully.

The star-kissed breeze that graced her form as she swung felt divine, like a friendly caress. Green eyes stared down over the brooch. The sight was certainly foreign, yet somehow...it felt completely proper.

She swung higher, turning her gaze to the sky and wondered what it must be like for her feathered companions, soaring freely every day, far out of reach from those threatening woods.

Before coming to a stop, Elunai pushed herself one last time up toward the daystar and reached a hand out as though she would grasp it. "One of these days..." she said, "I hope to shine like you."

The swing slowed to a halt and her hand rose again to feel of her own star. "I light the night...with relentless grit. I am the star that-"

A sudden, violent bang sounded around the corner of the cottage.

Elunai's head snapped up as she jumped off the swing. She watched Stryk spring to attention and head for the abode just as she forced herself forward. The girl flew around the garden porch, posture defensive.

There was no sign of movement...just a lone starling lying in shock on the pavement.

Breath left her as a thousand unwelcome thoughts invaded Elunai's mind all at once. Frantic, she looked around for Zeidys, but the paladin was still nowhere in sight.

The girl sank to her knees next to the bird, hesitant to reach out to the creature. Then, her voice returned, "Stryk...!" she called as the horse approached, "Where's Zei?!"

"She had an errand in the woods, but that was a while ago... I'm sure she'll be back soon," he said.

Iridescent feathers of beige-speckled black seemed to barely lift at the starling's shallow breathing. He couldn't move at all, not even to lift his head, but there were, again, no signs of outward harm.

One of Elunai's unstable hands ran through her hair, taking hold at the roots. Every failure up to that point began to weigh and fully convince her of her utter inability to do virtually anything.

Watchful eyes gathered under the apple tree at the commotion. The sparrows, Fehln, and Pikan filtered into the clearing with Remlli. The old rabbit had decided to make one of his rare, midday appearances to partake in the share of carnival squash.

"She still feels responsible..." he said quietly, not taking his tired eyes off of Elunai's distraught form. "Never saving a single life...might well be the end of hers one day."

Pikan turned to Remlli. "How many has she tried to save?" he asked.

The rabbit's ear twitched as he seemed to wrestle with his thoughts. "I've lost count. The dark-haired woman gave her that book to help hone her abilities after my son drowned."

The listening animals tensed while Fehln remained still, eyes trained on his human friend struggling under the horse's soft assurances. The albino had been there through her history of failed rescue attempts. He was acutely aware of how it killed her little by little each time, and...how there was nothing he could do about it.

"I'm so sorry..." Pikan said.

Remlli shook his head. "I wish I could say these deaths were natural. But none of them are. That's why she struggles as much as she does. Something...the curse, it seems...targets her with a steady, torturous form of pain."

Since his arrival at the glade, Pikan had begun to wonder about that suffering, but never knew for sure what was going on until then.

"If she doesn't learn to overcome it..." Fehln stopped himself from finishing that thought. "Well...I think that's why the other woman pushes her so hard."

They watched Elunai move to gather the starling into her wrap cape, as she'd done with so many other dying creatures. Pikan and the two sparrows suddenly lurched forward to accompany her back into he cottage as Fehln stood his ground.

Remlli glanced over at the squirrel, knowingly. The two had both been around long enough to know Fehln's words could not get through to her, no matter how much he wished they could, and his patience waned with his energy.

"You should at least go to her. If nothing else..." the rabbit coaxed.

Fehln glanced at the dirt about his paws and issued a slight nod. "Yeah..." he said. When he lifted his head, he found Stryk already looking over to him in anticipation.

Elunai reappeared in the doorway and sank to the threshold as Pikan, Phel, and Lei spoke tenderly to her.

She had wrapped the starling in soft linen and set him in a small crate with only a single, fervent prayer before following the book's guidance to grant the burdened soul a quiet respite.

"This is best for now, just let him rest..." Pikan told her.

Lei nodded. "You can watch him from a distance, Elunai...breathe."

Truthfully, Elunai was terrified to let the dark-feathered bird out of her sight. Knees slid up to her chest as trembling hands slipped back into her hair. "I need Zei...I need that potion from Jikyshu..." she whimpered.

"You need to calm down," came the familiar, squirrelly voice from between Stryk's ears.

Elunai's gaze shot up to the white animal, half panicked and half furious at his perceived lack of empathy.

That's when he saw the star on her chest. A curious sound made its way through Fehln's throat.

"*What...*" the girl forced.

"It's still not lit..."

"Of *course* it's not. I'm *not* what she thinks I am - proof!" She gestured at the lifeless jewel.

"Liar." Though he may not have possessed the ability to encourage her by any traditional means, Fehln's skill in riling the maiden's fiery spirit was unparalleled.

"Excuse me?!" she snapped.

"Just like you lied about wanting the curse to put you out of your misery that one night. You know for a straight fact this isn't who you are. What's with you, kid?"

Elunai's jaw hung agape as fear gave way to shock and anger. "Liar...?" her voice cracked. And yet, that was as far as she got before realizing his motive. The girl shut her mouth and gently grabbed for Stryk's outstretched muzzle. Her forehead rested against the bridge of the horse's nose as her thumbs slid over his dark, winter coat, no longer wanting to face the white one.

"Let's take our thoughts elsewhere for now, little one," the steed said quietly. "Maybe we can find that light."

"Elsewhere..." Elunai echoed in somewhat of a trance. "Zei wants me to leave this place. I don't really understand why."

Stryk lifted his muzzle and gave the girl's shoulder a quick tap. "Do you think it could have anything to do with the reason you've never left?" he asked.

Fehln watched the girl fall silent again and lean back from cradling the horse's nose.

Elunai felt her eyes start to wander back in the bird's direction before she stopped herself and refocused straight ahead. "Because...I'm afraid?"

Stryk issued a low sound in agreement.

"Why does that mean I should leave?" she asked.

"Could anything steeped in darkness ever bear light?" a feminine voice asked in response. Zeidys appeared from the far side of the garden, daystar rays playing off the silver edges of her tunic. "Could a life built on fear ever truly thrive?"

"Zei! The bird, it-"

"Answer the question, Elunai."

Elunai tensed at the older woman's sharpness. "It...could keep me alive..."

"For a time. Perhaps. Until it overstays its welcome...and summons death from within." Zeidys stopped at the edge of the stone patio and lowered the tip of her sheathed blade onto the stones. Noticing the brooch over the young woman's chest, her lips gave way to a faint smile that shone even more brightly in her eyes.

"Do you simply want to stay alive, dear one?" asked Stryk, "Or maybe...could you entertain the thought of *living*?" His voice slowed, drawing out that last word as though it was meant to permeate clear though every doubt.

Elunai's eyes roamed the length of Zei's weapon, tall and steadfast as it rested before her. Without even being drawn, the sword exuded a striking air of beauty, grace, and power, just like its owner. The girl's mind spun with the prospects of life and the words of those in front of her...even Fehln's.

What would that feel like...? To truly live. To believe, without a shadow of a doubt, that she was inherently *worthy* of such a life.

Maybe...

At the slight stirring of the starling behind her, Elunai finally looked back into the kitchen.

"Maybe..." she breathed, rising from the threshold.

All, save for the young maiden, noticed the subtle sparking of the Stelluvak Star at its edges.

The image of Zei's sword was still bright in Elunai's mind as she approached the crate. So many dark experiences...yet its light still burned. How?

The starling began trying to push itself up. The bird was silent in his suffering, but the girl knew how hard he struggled under the influence of the curse. His breathing labored. Still, she refrained from reaching out to him.

The sword, of course, never chose or questioned its purpose. An unfortunate human ability. But then...the ability to question and choose was still an ability. A power of sorts. *Her* power. And to dispel a ravaging hell within a soul...could that also...be chosen?

"Against all odds, against all logic, and at all costs...perhaps the only way to shine through darkness...is to choose the light anyway," she whispered. When the creature faltered again, Elunai took another step forward. "Yes, you *can*," she breathed.

The brooch sparked wildly in response.

Zei placed a hand on her hip as she watched, hazel eyes alight with anticipation.

Elunai placed her hands on either side of the crate. "If it burns in me, it burns in you, too, winged one. Let it through," she coaxed.

Slowly, the starling managed to rise to a semi-seated position, and Elunai gently picked up the crate. Moving back to the doorway, she set the makeshift nest at the edge of the entryway and sat beside it. From there, the bird lifted its head to the open sky.

"The flight is yours," she whispered.

The feathers on the bird's neck began to rise as its body leaned further upward. In the next moment, the starling leapt into the air.

With a shrill call, the onyx blur went soaring passed Stryk and Fehln, headlong into the firmament.

Elunai knew the creature was still fighting, but there it went...defying the pain amidst the daystar's rays. She watched it slowly disappear as a liquid blur overtook her line of sight.

The atmosphere seemed to shift as her companions began celebrating the triumph. Surreal elation filled Elunai's chest. Gratitude, relief, wonder, and then...a sense of displacement. That feeling, that sound, that sight...was foreign to her. She wasn't certain how to connect with it, what her next step should be, or if she should let it all continue.

She had saved a life.

As much as she'd wanted, prayed, and fought for it...she wasn't entirely sure what to make of the reality.

The maiden's gaze lowered to the southern path leading out from the clearing, catching a golden glint through the branches.

CHAPTER 13

The evening poured a warm light through the windows despite the hints of frost. Elunai stood staring at the quaint, empty satchel lying on her bed - the only travel sack she owned. The sensation of pins and needles pricked at her finger tips, and her heart raced and spun along with her thoughts. When she felt Zeidys's presence behind her, she let herself admit, "I feel lost..."

"In what way?" the older woman asked.

The girl let a silent moment pass in which she convinced herself to hide her confusion over her newfound light. She'd seen the brooch. Not a blazing example of what a star should be, but undoubtedly the makings of something new...something brighter. "I don't know what I should take...what I *can* take. I have no idea where I'm going or how to get there or what I'm going to do once I arrive. It all seems so foolish...and terrifying...and uncharted," she finally said.

"Then why have you decided to leave?"

Elunai drew in a deep breath and turned to meet Zeidys's eyes. "All of that nothing...out there...suddenly became everything."

"Freedom is a beautiful thing," Zeidys agreed. "Be mindful of what you take with you."

Curiosity painted over Elunai's expression.

"Avoid frivolous hindrances. You'll want to fill that bag only with what you truly need - body, mind, and soul." Zeidys turned to head upstairs, sending Elunai a final, sharp glance. "And that's *all* you'll be able to take with you."

A shaken breath left the girl's lungs as her eyes slightly widened.

As the paladin headed up to the loft, Elunai bounded out the front door, not bothering to grab a shawl or cape for warmth. She stopped short on the cobblestone at the base of the steps, staring breathless over at the huddle of animals gathered around the lit fire site. Hearing soft hoof-falls saunter up behind her, the girl asked,

"None of them?" She didn't take her eyes off the creatures before her. "Not one of them can come with me?"

"This is actually their home," the old horse responded. "Where they ultimately belong."

Elunai turned to him. "But how are you able to accompany Zei through the woods? I thought animals could come and go as they pleased...just like people. I don't understand."

"You know they can wander into the woods. But where you're headed, Elunai...they inherently aren't be able to follow."

She knew asking what that meant would be fruitless. Not a soul would ever explain that particular nuance of her journey. Every bone in her body began to ache for her to stay right where she was, to again believe that change was unnecessary, and to be at peace with never knowing what was on the other side of the wooded world.

However, something had already changed.

Ever since the Stelluvak Star found new life on her person, something had begun to feel...different...about her surroundings. If she were to put a word to it, perhaps it would be akin to 'cage.' The feeling made her heart restless. Even if her companions belonged in that place, Elunai was slowly starting to believe, deep in the confines of her spirit, that she did not.

With a shiver, the girl stepped back into the cottage momentarily to procure a wrap cape from the wall hook and a bucket of feed. The pale was a great deal heavier than usual with freshly harvested and intentionally stockpiled grains, but she hauled it all the way to the garden fire pit and set it at the edge of the emptied millet patch.

Her friends watched as she sat amongst them - not lifting her gaze to meet their expectant stares.

No one spoke for a long moment, each soul present deeply understanding the implications of the maiden's decision.

Lei and Phel sidled up to her first, followed by Miiskoe and Pikan.

Fehln then climbed up into the girl's lap and, subsequently, her tear-blurred field of vision.

"Elunai..." the albino said softly, "We know what it's costing you. I hope you're not second-guessing any of this. Listen...I know you don't take me seriously, but I'm proud of you, kid. I mean that. This was a long time coming."

She sucked in a sudden, unsteady breath she hadn't realized she'd been holding. Fehln's words loosed something in her that had been wound very tightly, although she still couldn't speak through the lump in her throat.

The squirrel continued, "Daystar Haven's a place of rest. No person, not even you...is meant to stay forever. Even so...you should know how you..." he paused a moment, an extra flicker of light dancing in his pastel eyes, "changed...this place."

The young woman squeezed her eyes shut, silent droplets wringing from their seams as she lowered her head to her friend's. Him and his stupid way with words.

Far on the edge of a distant memory, it was just them. All she remembered was dread and bewilderment before he'd found her alone in the glade. Nothing seemed quite as dismal after that.

"Dumb nut...makin' her cry more," Miiskoe shot. "Missy, you've got a whole future ahead of you. It's the right choice, leaving this place. No one would wanna spend forever with that overbearing halfwit anyway."

Fehln nearly retaliated before Pikan spoke, "Your kindness will stay 'ere with us y'know. That stuff doesn't disappear." In a bout of shyness, little paws rose to rub at that tiny muzzle again as the girl turned to him.

"That kind of light is permanent," Lei agreed.

Movement rustled at the garden's edge, and Elunai glanced up to find Remlli, the cardinals...and even Mister Coon waddling up under the apple tree to the fireside. The raccoon parked himself a farther distance away than the rest, but sat in silent solidarity nonetheless.

Remlli only nodded to the girl, words unneeded to convey his understanding and approval.

Wiping a few wet trails from her face, Elunai said, "There's enough food gathered to last you a good while...although I know you don't really need me for all that..."

"It's been appreciated," Mister Red assured her.

She went on to tell them about the provisions she'd made for future travelers and potential care plans for the cottage while she was away. Elunai knew they didn't have much control over the fate of the glade...but she couldn't simply abandon her home without a thought.

Time slowed as they remained there by the fire for a long while, conversing and reminiscing through starset. Zeidys tended to the lamps, as usual, but did not disturb the group of friends in the garden.

It wasn't until the girl began to shiver underneath her wrap cape that the creatures encouraged her to head inside and pack. Elunai knew she should, but her body felt completely rigid in resistance to the notion.

Fehln hopped off her lap and fished a small object out from the nearby bushes. When he returned, he motioned for her to hold out her hand and placed a lone acorn in her palm.

"You found...an oak?" she asked.

"It's pretty far out there, but it's massive. Old. But strong. I could tell its roots ran deep and its branches were hardened against the curse," the squirrel said. "Maybe you'll see it on your travels."

"Where is it?"

"South."

She closed her fingers over the acorn and stood to look out toward the southern entrance of the glade. Between the oak, the goldfinch, and Jikyshu's homeland, she knew which route she'd be taking. That was the most information she'd ever gathered for a future journey, and the prospect of such treasures hidden in the darkness again piqued her curiosity.

Her eyes scanned over the expanse of the clearing until they rested on the cottage, and she took in the entirety of the household she'd built up. The structure had been there. Bare-bones though it was on the horizons of her memory, she'd made that place into something any young woman could be proud of.

A shrill, inner voice cried as the maiden dared to step toward it again.

The last time...

Something in her chest jerked when her feet moved in the direction of the cottage and she looked back at the huddle by the fire.

Eyes wide and uncertain, Elunai held Fehln's steady gaze with hers. The entire moment felt like a dream. Surreal. And overwhelmingly heavy.

"Thank you..." she managed to whisper before darting for the doorway.

She'd wept enough. Any more, and she feared losing her resolve.

～ .⊹ ✧ ⊹. ～

It was nearly midnight.

Lamplight flickered dimly over the packed satchel on the bed, the oil in the metal basin nearly depleted. A few packages of food, medical and clothing provisions, her journal, the cup from Jikyshu, and the acorn from Fehln all rested snugly within the confines of the travel bag.

Elunai looked over at the book Zeidys had given her on the use of light-bearing abilities and noted how she finally felt she knew it by heart. There was a peace about leaving it with the cottage.

After one final sweep of the main room, the girl closed up the bag and set it on the dresser by her clothing for the next day's journey.

She couldn't bring herself to sleep in that bed one more time. The heaviness she felt even as she turned the lamp all the way down nearly brought her to her knees. Her heart was still begging her to not go through with the departure. But her spirit...that piece seemed to feel something else entirely.

In the dying light of the fireplace, Elunai made her way upstairs where Zeidys was already sleeping. It was strange to see the paladin in such a vulnerable state, and the girl felt a soft twinge of gratitude at the trust such a powerful person seemed to place in her.

The loft was warm with heat radiating from the chimney stones, and thus were the bed sheets. As she slid between them, slowly and quietly, those soft linens felt just like like the bath had - a most loving embrace...and she wondered just why she'd never slept up there in the winter before then.

As her cheek rested against the pillow, Elunai's mind threatened to take a dark path, pondering those winding woods...and what was waiting within. But then, her lips parted to a whisper, "I am the star...I'll keep it lit."

The words repeated over and over until at last, rest found her.

87

CHAPTER 14

Steady rays from the daystar beckoned Elunai back into the waking world the next morning.

Something was off.

The heat from the chimney had faded, and the cottage was uncharacteristically cold. A pit formed in the girl's stomach as consciousness fully returned and her thoughts shifted to the day.

With a pained groan, she twisted under the sheets and looked over at Zeidys's bed.

It was empty. Made. And there were no signs of the paladin's belongings anywhere.

One glance over at the small window revealed the first snowfall of the season had covered the glade overnight.

Elunai slowly sat up, pulling the covers closer against her chest. She stared out the frosted glass as light played off the tiny ice crystals in a sort of greeting. However, that wasn't the cheerful, lazy, wintery hello she remembered from years past. Something wanted her up.

She had half the mind to simply stay put - to revel in the remaining heat of that final night's rest for a moment longer. And that's when the knot pulsed in her gut.

Elunai doubled over, swinging her legs over the side of the bed.

There would be no lingering. No reveling. She had to go.

Pulling the top blanket from the bed, she wrapped it around her figure to keep warm as she made her way downstairs.

"Zei...?" she called quietly.

The fireplace wasn't lit. The small home was completely silent.

Glancing out the large, front room window, she saw no one. Not Zeidys, nor Stryk. No sight of Fehln, or even a hint of paw prints in the snow. Everything was still...as though the entire glade had frozen in time. The only sign of life was the shining of the daystar on sparkling, white ground.

She waited. Fehln's fluffy tail was bound to burst out from the cold at any moment, covered in snowflakes that matched his coat.

As the minutes crawled, Elunai's heart chilled with the world around her.

Where was everyone...?

Copper and blonde whipped about her face as the girl looked around the cottage, desperate for some sign that she was awake...alive, even.

Everything was so quiet, so still. Her breath hitched and shallowed.

Dropping the blanket, she ran to the front door and swung it open to be met with more of the same atmosphere, only colder. No sounds. No movement.

"Zei...? Fehln?" she called once again.

No response.

Elunai pushed herself back into the house, closing the door, and leaning her forehead against its carved, wooden panels. Her heaving shoulders and quickened breath were the only sight and sound she beheld. Heavy puffs of condensation poured from her lips as her head spun.

"Come on..." she told herself, "Come *on*..."

And, finally, she had every reason to leave.

Without even bothering with the fireplace, Elunai turned to her bedroom, catching herself from stumbling on the way.

Something hard and sharp fell to the floor as she grabbed the set of warm clothing from atop her dresser.

A strained, green gaze roved over the dimming brooch before she bent to pick it up. Dimming...but not dead. She set the star back upon the dresser, staring at it as though it was the last glimmer of hope in existence while she dressed in long sleeves, pants, and a tunic.

Fetching the last bit of oil she owned, Elunai filled the lantern Zeidys had set on the kitchen table only days before. A quick flint strike later, and it burned in rebellion to the threatening stillness. She let herself stare at the flame a moment, lingering against its rising heat.

"I wonder why she left me a lantern…when she doesn't carry one out there herself," the girl thought aloud.

As she gathered a bit of breakfast from the cupboards, Elunai grew more aware of just how *dead* everything felt. Sights, smells, textures, and motions once familiar to her were somehow hollow and devoid of meaningful connection. Colors seemed to mute, and her eyesight blurred slightly at how detached she felt from her surroundings. Her once warm and inviting home was becoming all but foreign right in front of her.

Confused and disturbed, the girl couldn't even sit to eat. "Zei…why?" she whispered, bringing a piece of apple to her mouth. As she ate, her hands occasionally wandered over to the lantern's glass, again taking in its warmth. She stared into the glow the same way she had the brooch, her body begging for relief from the tension she felt.

That's when Zei's words filtered back through her mind.

'I'm not leaving until you decide who you want to be.'

Well, Elunai had certainly made her decision. She just couldn't figure out why the paladin had to take everything alive along with her on the way out.

Cold well water washed down the maiden's throat, and she breathed deeply in between gulps. Setting the cup down, she let out a long sigh followed by another, full intake of air.

In truth, she realized, if everyone had still been around…leaving would have been exponentially more difficult.

"Keep it lit." A renewed sense of urgency came over her, and Elunai turned back to the bedroom. She had to get out of there. The longer she lingered, the more uncomfortable everything became.

The satchel strap was pulled over her head and rested diagonally over her torso, followed by her favorite, white wrap cape with blue trim. The brooch was secured into place - its light just ever so slightly brighter than earlier. Boots, gloves, and a cerulean scarf were donned last.

Snatching the lantern off the table and the staff from the doorframe…the young woman took in one final, deep breath and headed out the door.

The iron latch clicked shut behind her.

Elunai's grip about the lantern's handle tightened as she finally heard a new sound.

Wind.

Faint...but there was definitely a light whistling coming from the southern forest border. Somehow, it seemed like a call - a merciful summon so as not to leave her faltering in the weight of what she was about to do. Alone.

Despite the wooded whispers, there was no movement in the trees. No birds chirping in the air. Not a single creature scurrying about the haven. She couldn't even hear the babbling of the brook, ironically - it had chosen *then*, of all times, to be silent.

For a moment, Elunai wondered if the air she was breathing was merely in her imagination.

One last look.

The apple tree seemed nearly dead with most of its leaves fallen, standing alone without the wildlife about to enjoy its branches. A memory of its vivid life struck Elunai hard, causing her heart to ache and her feet to move...straight for the southern path.

Her footsteps were light despite how heavy she felt, landing exactly where she knew the larger stones lay beneath the smooth snow cover.

The soft crunching under her boots halted with her at the edge of all she had feared for as long as she could remember. Her gaze lifted all the way up to the top of the towering, darkened trees looming over her small form. She was just out of their reach...just inside the haven where the daystar still poured its light. In a way...her actions felt like surrender.

What if it was all a ruse? A massive, elaborate plan conjured by the darkness to get her to give in to it...?

But then...what else was there for her to do? Especially then...

Holding up the lantern, Elunai did her best to shed even the faintest bit of light onto the pathway leading away from the clearing.

No use. The shadow swallowed any form of light that dared enter. Honestly, what was the *point* of that lantern?

The pace of her heart quickened. Glancing over at the stream on her left, Elunai could tell it was still flowing south even though she couldn't hear it. At least she might have some semblance of a companion as she plunged herself into the unknown.

On the count of three, the girl made to move forward...but her legs froze in place - not due to any fault of winter's.

Her breath rate rose, too, as she stared ahead, willing herself to move. "Please..." she whispered into the void. "Set me free..."

As if on cue, the glimmer of the goldfinch flashed into view from above.

The ethereal bird descended the tree tops and soared down the path she was to take through the wooded world. Somehow, the shadow did not seem to overcome it.

Watching the fading trail of its light retreating farther into the forest, Elunai called out, "Wait...!"

She suddenly noticed a sparkling, golden feather resting on the ground before her, not far beyond the tree line. Gripping her staff even more tightly, Elunai lifted one foot out of the snow and inched it toward her newfound sign of hope on the road ahead.

As she shifted her weight to slip beyond the old wooden lampposts and into the shadows, something else seemed to shift with her.

Shock filled Elunai's chest as she looked down and beheld what appeared to be the rays from the daystar...moving right along with her!

The path around the girl's feet should have been devoid of life. Instead, it was illuminated with a warm, inviting glow emanating from above her.

Looking up, her viridian gaze confirmed there was indeed no light making it through the canopy of branches overhead. In wonder, she took another step. The light followed suit. Then another.

The maiden didn't know how, but the daystar was actually defying the curse in her midst. Not a hint of malignant intent neared those brilliant beams about her.

Glittering green eyes fixed on the ground in front, and she wondered if the miracle would cease if she dared look away.

As Elunai reached the place where the feather fell, it dissipated, almost as though the daystar rays were absorbing it. Finally, looking ahead, the girl caught sight of yet another feather further down the path. Her wonder took hold, and Elunai found herself traveling deeper and deeper into the wooded world...not once looking back at the fading glade that had been her home.

CHAPTER 15

One, slow step at a time.

Hours passed...and the only light to be seen was that which enveloped Elunai from the unseen aether, her lantern, the struggling Stelluvak Star, and the single, mysterious feathers that kept appearing just before her. The trees seemed to devour the rest of her surroundings in thick twists and tangles that hardly allowed for any deviation from the pathway, which twisted and tangled in kind.

How could any place in existence exude so much silence and dread without being death itself...? And why would anyone in their right mind willingly traverse it?

Even the soft sounds of her footfalls were nearly too much for her to bear in that place. She wished they would silence as well, lest anything decided to drown out the light that kept her safe.

Compounding the suffocating atmosphere was the incessant tug of exhaustion the girl had begun to feel as she trudged forward without any indication of when she may see or find anything in that endless abyss.

'*A lot of trees*,' she remembered Jikyshu describing. A lot *indeed*.

Her eyes darted in the direction of the stream. She couldn't see it any longer, but held to a fleeting hope that it may still be there, traveling with her. She swallowed, attempting to sate a drying throat as her shoulder shifted under the weight of the satchel.

How she longed for the lighter, warmer weight that used to grace that shoulder. Thoughts slowly turning to a certain albino companion, Elunai moved the staff to her lantern-bearing hand so she could search the bag at her side. Once she felt the acorn, she gripped it tightly, bringing it out into view as she continued to walk.

The sight of the small fruit with its dried, little cap caused a bit of the surrounding light to seep into her core. Warm...soothing. A much welcome distraction from the hellish nightmare of a thicket.

"Fehln..." she whispered, "you must've traveled a long time to find this. Where is that-"

Elunai looked up.

"Tree..."

The disorienting path suddenly gave way to a vast clearing, and Elunai stopped when the dirt road faded under a covering of dead leaves.

There, in the center of the clearing, was the most colossal tree she had ever seen. Its trunk towered above the surrounding woods and splayed branches out beyond her line of sight. That had to be the oak Fehln spoke of.

To Elunai's wonder, the expanse wasn't quite as dark as the rest of the forest, but where the soft illumination was coming from, she couldn't tell. The maiden stood there a moment in silent awe, unaware that her own breath had faltered. The sudden need to breathe again revived her remaining senses with it.

Elunai began frantically searching for the next feather.

None appeared.

Swallowing again to sooth both her nerves and her throat, she placed the acorn back inside the satchel and dared to move forward, the mystical light of the daystar still providing strength and protection. Despite the dissipated pathway, Elunai headed straight out into the clearing toward the gargantuan oak. As she moved closer, her eyes began to make out large forms congregating at its base. Her pace slowed.

Gradually, the light revealed an extension of bark. More twisted trunks, big enough to completely dwarf her in size...but they weren't trees. Drawing even nearer, the girl realized she was looking at the oak's roots.

They whipped and swirled in every direction, weaving in and out of the ground as though they had once been alive and then had frozen.

Stretching her lantern up and out as far as she could, Elunai stepped through the winding runners along the leaf-strewn dirt until she came upon a giant section of root that blocked her way ahead.

The bark was so old it seemed dead, falling apart in nearly petrified chunks. She couldn't see around it, but desperately wanted to get to the large trunk at the center of the clearing. Fehln had procured that acorn recently, which meant there was growth left somewhere on that tree. If there was any spark of life in that place, Elunai had to find it. Perhaps it would signal a way out of there.

The girl's hand extended to just barely brush the root with a gloved finger. When nothing came of it, she pressed her palm against the cold surface. It was rough, but it was solid. She then brought her boot up to a vertical scar in the wall that had rotted out, forming a short of shelving. A few pieces of wood fell out at the impact, but she was able to get some footing on the ledge.

Elunai looked up to gauge the crumbling rift and decided it would get her high enough to climb up over the root. So, swinging the staff across her shoulders, the girl hooked the lantern onto one end of it, slid the handle to a secure position, stabled herself against the bark, and lifted off the forest floor.

The act of focusing all her attention on not falling seemed to take her mind off the foreboding woods around her, giving Elunai the strength she needed to balance and climb with only one free hand.

Her movements were slow, just as they had been the whole way through the winding forest. Exhaustion aside, Elunai needed absolute assurance that each move she made wasn't going be her last. Acute awareness and calculated steps were of utmost priority...which, ironically, added to her fatigue.

Halfway to the top. She glanced up at the oak's canopy in growing anticipation of what was waiting on the other side.

A sound crack reverberated below her foot.

Elunai registered the branches far above begin to recede as her body swayed in backward descent. That free hand shot out to grab at the next jagged chunk of wood, which gave way as her foot broke through the shelf below her.

Her body twisted, desperate to grab onto something, anything!

The slightest, raspy cry escaped the girl's throat just as the staff caught between the woody rift and an adjacent root.

Her one hand clung hard to the hefty rod while the other clasped her mouth shut, eyes frantically scanning the surrounding area for any sign of movement.

A long moment passed. Nothing else seemed to shift, and all went quiet as the bark settled again.

Her breath gradually slowed with her heartbeat, and Elunai's feet reoriented amidst the scar in the root wall.

"Great...daystar..." She shuddered and pressed her whole body against the perch.

The staff and lantern were recovered as soon as she got herself up above them on a sturdier shelf, and the climb resumed the rest of the short way to the apex of the rift.

Elunai paused near the top and reached her free arm over the curvature of the root, taking in one more deep breath. The air left her slowly, sending ripples of petrified dust rolling across the surface of the bark as she readied her move.

With a final heave, the girl pulled herself and all of her belongings up over the crest and brought her legs up to kneel atop it, the daystar rays warming the hard surface beneath her.

Green eyes widened at the sight of what lay beyond.

She could see the oak's foundation, finally. But just before that, a mass of roots of varying size twisted about to form a large archway over the ground, nearly a complete circle, between her and the trunk. And although it was still a ways off from where she was, Elunai could see a faint, yet revealing glow emanating from the cracks in the structure's bark.

"What...is-" she whispered as something else caught her eye.

There was the stream she thought she'd lost, still silent, yet running faithfully throughout the horde of roots. The water flowed straight through the center of the arch and then forked around the oak's trunk as though it existed solely to serve that tree.

Somehow, the first thought that crossed Elunai's mind at seeing the brook was a wonder of whether her laundry soap had actually poisoned the fish *and* the old oak tree. She silently cursed at Fehln for ever spewing that nonsense.

The dryness in her throat shifted her mind to another idea.

Looking down off the ledge in front of her, Elunai decided against jumping from the large root she sat atop. Over to the left, another wooden appendage wound around her perch and descended at a much more gradual rate toward the ground.

Finally, she stood.

Her movements were again slow and calculated, but there was something different about how she carried herself. Perhaps it was the trend in her security or the prospect of satiated thirst and progress, but Elunai lowered herself onto the adjacent root with just a bit more surety in her step.

She was able to walk upright all the way back to the forest floor, only tilting and swaying slightly to balance over the curvature of the root. And the girl could have sworn, if only slightly, that the glow of the arch ahead brightened as she drew nearer.

Though the atmosphere was still heavy with darkness, there was no threat, no sign of malice present amidst the throng of oak wood. The clearing was somehow far less suffocating than the path that had led her there.

And so, when she reached the stoney edge of the quietly slithering stream, Elunai lowered her lantern with the staff to the ground and sat to rest.

An ache crept through her back and legs as she finally registered how stiff she had gone over those long hours of trekking through the forest. Her gaze roved over the surrounding area, taking in the stillness and the mysterious wooden arch towering overhead. She briefly wondered if the goldfinch lived there with the giant oak. Perhaps it had something to do with the warm glow she beheld under that bark. Maybe she was supposed to do something with it?

The arch stood only a few feet away from where she had stopped, just as quiet and old as its surroundings, and its subtle light seemed gently inviting. In a moment, Elunai decided, she would inspect that strange bark. But first...

Gloves were removed, and dipping a finger into the trickling waters of the stream, the girl felt that it was as cool as she remembered it from the haven. The waters that passed under the light of her lantern and daystar rays revealed that the brook was still clean and clear. And, if she listened closely, she could hear it faintly whispering around her finger.

There were no fish or any other creatures for that matter. Just the lonely stream itself carrying on its way as it always did.

Elunai's hands cupped and plunged wholly into the crisp liquid, scooping out a tiny pool from which she leaned in to drink.

The water was good. *Divinely* so.

Turning more fully toward the stream, the maiden reached into her satchel to bring out the single, ceramic cup in her possession. Those gilded blossoms gleamed brilliantly in the concentrated daystar light as she ran the cup across the water's surface, filling it to the brim. She brought the refreshment to her lips and only sipped at first. Then, her head tilted back as she drank and drank, hardly stopping for air, eyes slipping shut. She hadn't realized how parched she'd become.

Her back heaved as she finished with soft panting just barely audible over the surrounding silence. As she caught her breath, Elunai opened her eyes and found that she had trouble adjusting her vision again. And it was...colder?

Then...somehow...everything seemed darker.

Elunai glanced at the lantern that sat next to her, still alight. And that's when her eye caught the difference about her own form.

The daystar's rays...were gone.

Her blood went cold.

Pins and needles ran up the length of the girl's arms and legs as she froze in place, only using her strained eyes to scan the vicinity.

Then, she felt it - that sinister weight, the likes of which she could never fully describe in human words. The kind of evil that seeps into the core of living beings and makes them fear, not for their mortal life...but for their very soul.

Ever so slowly, the girl set the cup on the ground beside her.

As swiftly as her numbing legs could, she kicked off the large river rock next to her and rolled away from the stream just as a dark apparition came crashing down over the spot she'd occupied.

The sound of breaking ceramic and glass filled her ringing ears as both the drink ware and lantern obliterated. Not a hint of flame was left.

The dark form had no structure. No sound. Yet the girl's head pounded as though it was screaming at her.

Weak...suffer... she perceived over and over and over, straight into her mind.

Like an organic cloud of pure blackness, the monstrosity lunged for her again, kicking up a whirlwind of leaves just as another came from behind...and the side!

Elunai scrambled to her feet, all but throwing herself in the direction of the arch. She lurched and twisted in attempt to evade the tornadic projections that reached for her.

As soon as the girl's hand grasped one of the roots swirling about the arch, the brooch on her chest flashed in response to whatever light seeped through those wooden veins. Nothing else seemed to happen, though, and she

didn't have time to ponder the implications.

Foreign, unearthly rage pulsed through her senses as the phantoms became erratic in their pursuit. Elunai's blurred vision made her dizzy as she ran, just like it always tended to in the presence of the curse. Sheer will propelled the girl toward the gargantuan, center tree - still with no idea what she should do when she got there. All she knew in that moment was desperation.

As darkness incarnate whirled and turned over and around her, Elunai ducked and spun in every direction, just barely escaping its grasp. One small slip, and a tendril of black tore at the fabric around the Stelluvak Star, nearly ripping it off Elunai's cape before she fell headlong into the writhing stream.

Cold.

So, very, *very* cold.

The girl's senses suddenly reignited as the freezing sensation jolted her system. Still underwater, she noticed the brooch begin to brighten...and the blackened fabric around it. She finally registered just what the curse had tried to do.

The current was pushing her toward the oak when she surfaced, gasping for air. As the stream bent to curve around the vastness of the trunk, Elunai grabbed hold of a thinner root strand on the bank closest to the tree and hauled herself out of the water. She crawled up the bank and scrambled to her feet, making another run for the tree - cold be damned.

Before she could reach the oak, a wave of venom and hate came crashing down around her.

"*I* light the night!" she shouted.

The brooch responded again to her spirit, halting the phantoms in the surrounding air.

Elunai breathed heavily, watching the swirling manifestations of evil encircling her. There were so many of them then, it looked like a massive wall of shadow. Their deep, eternal hatred, though she did not understand it, surged deep through her senses and tainted every thought with despair.

The star's light faltered only slightly.

"I am the-" She felt the weight in her bones. There was no sensation on her skin, but her entire being began to suffocate as an unseen force killed her windpipe, weakened her body, and brought her to the ground.

The the rest of the maiden's light extinguished as she found herself unable to struggle...unable to move in any way. There was a weight on top of her like an iron blanket she couldn't see, pinning her flat.

Elunai looked to the oak as her vision began to fade. A somehow even darker form was moving toward her then, nearly human-shaped, but with...wings? Like the others, it did not make a sound, but she knew wholeheartedly that it meant to end her, body and soul.

Unable to move, breathe, or make a single sound, the spirit behind those glassy, viridescent irises unleashed its final cry into the abyss for anyone...anything to hear.

The winged phantom reached for her.

She felt the warmth first.

A white light from above filtered into view.

And then...peace.

A peace that wholly covered and dissipated all traces of weight bearing down from atop and within.

Gradually, Elunai registered the tears streaming across her face and the plume of golden feathers that had settled over her form.

Breath came, and then the strength in her limbs.

Slowly, the maiden pushed herself to a seated position over her legs where she bent, clinging to her own arms.

A gentleness cradled her mind even as she looked up and beheld the darkness still surrounding her. The hoard had stopped moving again, warded by the very presence of that mysterious bird.

Like the phantoms, the goldfinch did not make a sound, but she could certainly feel it. Elunai sensed the subtle, yet commanding power exuding from the small creature hovering just above her -

and the unparalleled life it gave. Just like the daystar.

The bright creature began to ascend again. The light began to lift as well, and even as the warmth slowly faded, Elunai still could not perceive the fear she had felt before.

"I..." she started with a soft breath, feeling her throat fully release, "I've got you." Hands with renewed vigor gripped harder against opposite arms as the maiden watched that gleaming tail flicker up through the oaken canopy. "You're safe." Her gaze lowered back to the apparitions just as the light faded and they launched. "I am not alone."

The Stulluvak Star illuminated anew, and that time, another source of brightness erupted from behind Elunai in tandem.

Just as she turned, the wall of malice closed her in and shrouded whatever had appeared in the forest. No sooner had the barrier settled was it suddenly sliced through with a blinding rift from the oak side.

Forcing through the dark mass of cloud was an armor-clad Zeidys - her sword alight. "You have to get over there!" she shouted.

Elunai could hardly hear above the whirring of wind and debris, yet found herself battling an onslaught of emotion. She looked back one more time at where the clearing had lit up. "What *is* that?!" she asked.

"Do you have the lantern?!" Zeidys asked, reaching the girl.

"No, it was destroyed!"

A tick of irritation crossed the paladin's expression before her blade glowed once again with a hot, orange heat. She flung a hard gust of that energy in the direction of the arch, and every dead leaf in its path burst into flame.

The sudden rise of firelight caused the apparitional wall to part in a frenzy above it, and Elunai could finally see that the root arch had framed a vortex of powerful, white light. The sound of metal again cutting through air drew her attention back.

Zeidys whipped her sword about in a circular motion over her head, generating a different kind of wind that carried with it wisps of white spark from the blade, effectively threatening the enemy's advance. "That," she said, "is your way out of here!"

"To where?!"

"Elunai...!" a deeper voice sounded.

Turning again, Elunai nearly lost her breath at the sight of Mister Keamotus and Jikyshu both fighting their way to the arch on the other side of the stream. Rather than packs or equipment, they held what looked like weapons of war, as bright as Zeidys's, as they engaged their own slew of phantoms.

Keamotus reached the swirling light first. He raised his arm high in a gesture for Elunai to follow, swung his battle axe to the rear to stave a final, hellbent tendril, and then disappeared into the vortex.

"What're you waiting for?! Let's go!" Jikyshu called over the chaos.

"Hey!" Elunai made to move for him, reaching out instinctively as a black mist descended on him.

The man's spear pierced through the air and erupted with a flash of radiance as it clashed with the apparition. Even as he ran and fought, he extended his hand to her. "This way!"

"You coming?" the girl asked, eyeing Zeidys.

In the midst of her efforts, the paladin met Elunai's frantic gaze. Steadfast and bright, those hazel eyes rivaled the daystar itself. "You first." Her lips curled up ever so slightly. "Move."

All at once, the entire forest seemed to roar with unnatural, horrifying depth as the winged phantom crashed against Zeidys's weapon, forcing her off her footing.

"*Now*, Elunai...!" she commanded.

The girl spun and bounded for the stream.

More apparitions appeared around her, but the star on her chest resisted their direct advance.

"I *will* keep it lit..." she attested through gritted teeth.

The phantoms suddenly burrowed beneath the ground around her and rocked the very foundations of the woods.

Elunai stumbled just as the clouded form burst back up through the dirt to swallow her whole.

With a fierce cry, the girl leapt off the rising rubble and hurled herself onto a low root that bridged over the stream. She slipped, ramming her shoulder hard against the wood, but adrenaline forced her back up to propel across the pass, the deathly shroud clawing at her heels.

A human hand grabbed hers as she reached the opposite bank, and Jikyshu launched into an all out sprint toward the arch with Elunai in tow.

"I can't take you through with me, you have to do this on your own!" he explained, "but you *can* do this!"

"How? Where does it lead?!"

"Decide on that now!" The man actually smiled in the midst of hell. He let go of her hand as they reached the portal and turned fully toward her, that caring glance of his laced with sincerity. "Come on, light bearer...they've kept you here long enough. Let's get you where you belong," he said. And before she could blink, the brightness consumed him.

"Jikyshu...!" Her peripheral grew dark as the curse closed in - she was out of options. Elunai glanced out at Zeidys one last time, eyes going wide at what she beheld before letting the light's power pull her through.

The warrior had finally let her own wings free to unleash the whole of heaven's fury on the demon before her. A triumphant grin plastered clear across her face, she asked the vanishing young maiden...

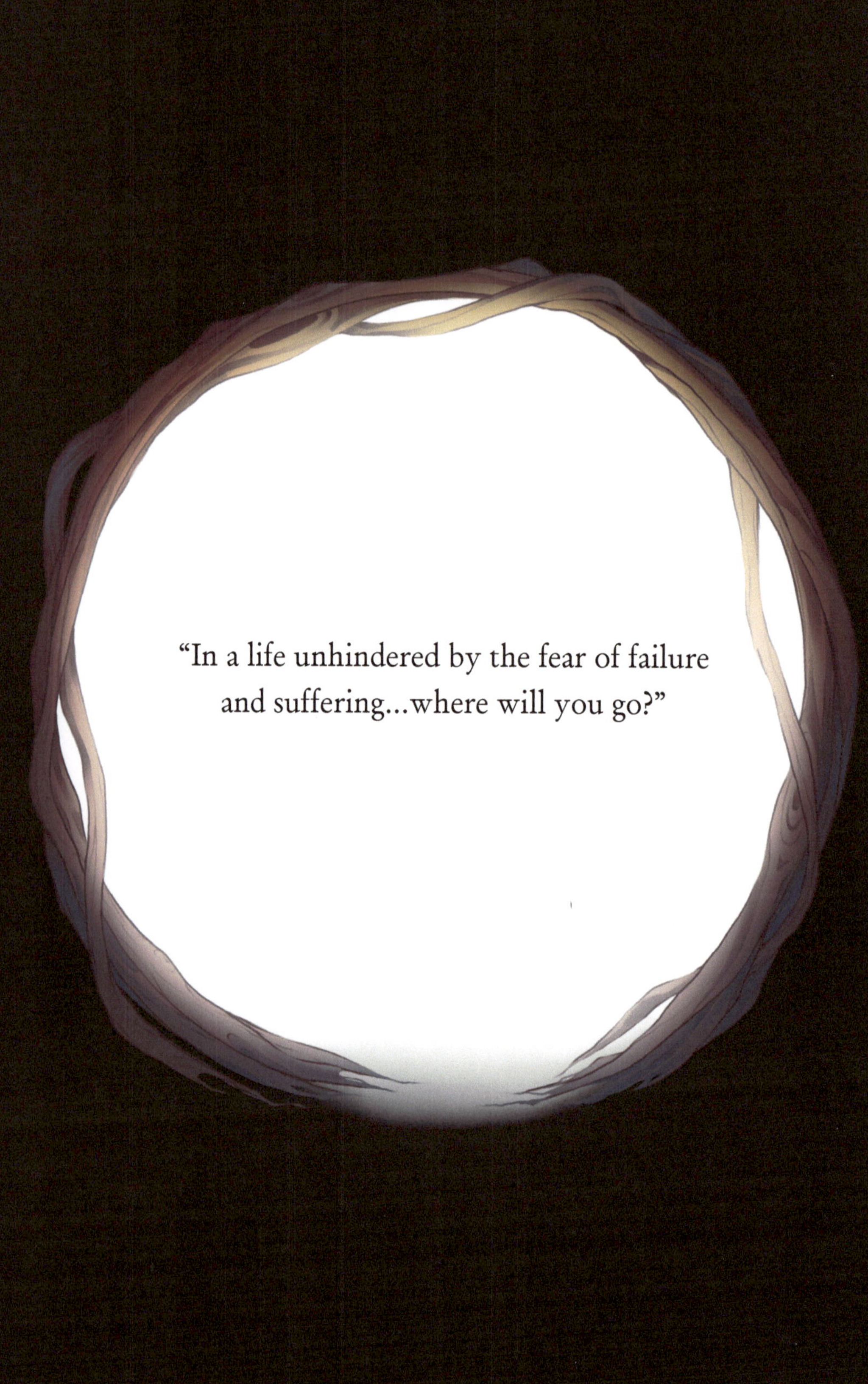
"In a life unhindered by the fear of failure
and suffering...where will you go?"

The end of the beginning of Elunai's tale ~

ACKNOWLEDGMENTS

If I'd never joined the military, my skills as an artist and author would never have waned. Evidence suggests my dream to weave purposeful stories for a living would've come to fruition a lot sooner had I continued to focus my time and energy on my creative calling instead of the call to national defense. I likely would not have experienced the mental health challenges I have, developed the chronic illnesses that degrade my daily quality of life, or faced my hardest days away from any semblance of a loved one. And if I'd never joined the military...I wouldn't be nearly as equipped to face the rest of this life as I am. I wouldn't have ever ventured out to experience and glean from as many different countries and cultures I have. I don't think I ever would have known the fulfillment of moving mountains globally - of watching the tangible, positive impacts of my team unfold across the planet in ways only a very small percentage of human beings ever get to. I promise you, if it wasn't for the military, I never would have attained the master's degree in Executive Leadership I did that set the foundation for my life as an entrepreneur. I wouldn't have met the most amazing souls in the most unlikely places who would end up as my second family and inspire me like no one anywhere else ever could. I also may not have been so thoroughly taught what kind of person and leader I should never aspire to be and what it's like to hold ground under immense, external pressure. Definitely would never have experienced war on a tactical level and shown just what caliber of hard things I'm truly capable of. Without breaking all the way down to rock bottom multiple times in a career that needed me to be the complete opposite... I don't think I ever would've been so humbled as a human being to learn the compassion and empathy that I have for those who suffer in that way - let alone how to ask for help again. And I doubt I would have come to realize what it is I truly need to help others with through my creative work. Without the military, I wouldn't have been able to invest in this new venture like I have, nor would I have been granted the invaluable honor of support and community with fellow veterans and service members for the rest of my days. So, I must first thank my Creator for closing the doors He did so the right ones could open when and how they needed to. He taught the lessons, brought the provision, held me through every lonely night, and gave me the miracles I never deserved - all while molding me into the person I needed to be at my core. And then I want to thank my brothers and sisters in arms... for training, strengthening, challenging, encouraging, correcting, supporting, mentoring, inspiring, and believing in me. Our time serving together will forever remain one of my greatest treasures. I am in awe of you every day and am able to sleep at night in the assurance that our armed forces are filled with people like you.

Additionally, thank you to my parents for your role in this book's existence. Your support throughout my military and now my creative endeavors has been critical to the journey. Mom, those late-night phone calls, even from across the world, saved so much more than my peace mind. And, Dad, your encouragement on the officer side of things kept me going under seemingly impossible circumstances. Leaving active duty and a stable lifestyle was one of the hardest things I've ever done, but knowing I had a place to call home on the other side provided the healing and freedom I needed discover who I'm meant to be. Love you always ~

I'm also deeply grateful to you, Shey. Six years of loving through each other's antics has to count for something. Thank you for believing in my ability to make this happen and your encouragement to stick with this intense dream of mine even when it meant we had to change our future plans pretty significantly. I've told you time and time again that your patience and grace are not lost on me, and I'm deeply grateful I get to share this adventure with you...even from afar. You'll always be my favorite ~

Likewise, there are incredible women around the world I crossed paths with in such times and places that rendered their influence like the hand of God itself pulling me up from beneath the waves. Sarah Miller, you're one of the best. The Spirit moves powerfully when you pray, you're one of the toughest fighters I know, and I'm forever grateful for your friendship and wise counsel. Absolutely cannot wait to witness this new writing warrior trajectory! Additionally, Christine Reyes, Theresa Alsip, Sande Cromer, Lisa Doyle, Brenda Cordle, Priscilla Malkin, Tammy Kinder-Tims, Candace Rowe, Jessica Hurtado, and Rachel LeVine - your advice, care, and mentorship grew and healed me in ways that paved the foundations for this kind of story and will have a lasting, domino-effect kind of impact for ages to come. Thank you so much for being who you are!

Here's to turning chapters...
Until I write again, best wishes on your journey ~

✧

ABOUT THE AUTHOR

CELEBRATING 30 YEARS OF CREATION~!

UNIesque is a professional artist returning to her storytelling roots after several years of active duty military service. Her creative journey ignited in 1996 with a passion for capturing life experiences via imaginative, illustrated narratives. Four years later, when 5th grade classmates discovered her secret ability to bring the imagined to life, the young creative decidedly found where she fit in the world, and empowering lives through art and storytelling became her mission. Personal experience and divine inspiration continue to shape the nature of her craft through the ages.

You're invited to delve into the making of this tale, experience the weaving of new adventures, and connect with fellow travelers on a journey to pursue the starlight of life at www.uniesque.com!

www.ingramcontent.com/pod-product-compliance
Lightning Source LLC
Chambersburg PA
CBHW061032100726
47911CB00006B/161